THE AMERICAN CIVIL WAR

A HOUSE DIVIDED

Edward F. Dolan

The Millbrook Press   Brookfield, Connecticut

Photographs courtesy of Corbis-Bettmann: cover, pp. 7, 8, 23, 28, 45, 56, 65; Culver Pictures: title page, pp. 31, 37, 52, 57, 72, 83; North Wind Picture Archives: pp. 13, 89 (both).

Library of Congress Cataloging-in-Publication Data
Dolan, Edward F., 1924–
The American Civil War: A House Divided/Edward F. Dolan.
p.   cm.
Includes bibliographical references and index.
Summary: An account of the Civil War from its causes to its final battles, including discussions of dominant figures of the era, strategies of major battles, and brutal sieges that marked this conflict.
ISBN 0-7613-0255-7 (lib. bdg.)
1. United States—History—Civil War, 1861–1865—Juvenile literature.
[1. United States—History—Civil War, 1861–1865.]   I. Title.
E468.D64
973.7—dc21   97-6995   CIP   AC

Published by The Millbrook Press, Inc.
2 Old New Milford Road
Brookfield, Connecticut 06804

CONTENTS

Fort Sumter Under Fire

The United States soldiers on sentry duty at Fort Sumter heard the sudden thump of a distant howitzer. They saw a glowing red dot rise through the predawn darkness. It arced toward them, growing larger as it came, and then fell to burst above their heads. They ducked low as shell fragments flew in all directions.

The time was 4:30 in the morning of April 12, 1861. The howitzer had just loosed what was to be the first shot in a war that would tear the United States apart. The fighting would pit the states of the North against those of the South, family against family, and friend against friend. Hate and sorrow would reign everywhere for four long years.

It was a war that had been brewing throughout the 1800s over a number of problems, chief among them the Southern practice of slavery. Many Northerners wanted to see it abolished, while the South insisted that slave labor was necessary to harvest its vast cotton crop, a crop that enriched the economy of the entire country. Southern anger over the matter reached a peak in late 1860 and caused seven states to secede from the Union—first South Carolina, and then Alabama, Florida, Georgia, Louisiana, Mississippi, and Texas.

In February 1861, these states joined to form a new nation—the Confederate States of America, or, as it was also called, the Confederacy—and named Jefferson Davis of Mississippi as its first president. Then, to give life to their infant country and equip it with an army, they began seizing the U.S. properties within its borders.

There were some 125 soldiers at Fort Sumter in Charleston, South Carolina. In the past weeks, they had heard reports of how U.S. forts, arsenals, and shipyards were being taken over throughout the seceded states. The takeovers had all been bloodless. At the time, President James Buchanan had been serving his last days in the White House after Abraham Lincoln's successful bid for the presidency in the November 1860 election. Not wanting to trigger a war during those final days, Buchanan had let all the facilities go without a fight.

Now, as dawn approached on this April 12, 1861, the men knew that only two Federal forts remained to be taken. One was a tiny post in Florida. The other was their own Fort Sumter.

Tension at Fort Sumter

Sumter stood on a sandbar at the entrance to Charleston's harbor. Named for General Thomas Sumter, who led a guerrilla force in the Revolutionary War, it was a five-sided brick building that in 1861 was still under construction.

With only a few cannons for their defense, the Sumter troops were tense. Trouble was certain to come their way soon. Their fellow post, Fort Moultrie over on the Charleston shore, had passed into Confederate hands along with a series of smaller installations around the harbor. Any day now, they would surely be ordered to give up Sumter. But would their commander, Major Robert Anderson, obey? Would he quietly surrender the last Federal bastion in Charleston? If not, would they be attacked? If attacked, they would not be able to hold out for long. Their guns were no match for the surrounding Confederate artillery. And their food supply was fast running out.

SUNSET VIEW OF FORT SUMTER BEFORE THE BOMBARDMENT

This etching shows Fort Sumter as it was before the first shot of the Civil War was fired upon it.

They could see but one ray of hope: Abraham Lincoln. When the Illinois lawyer had been sworn in as president a few weeks before—in early March—he had delivered an inaugural address that spoke to the Confederate states in friendly terms. He had urged them to return to the Union, saying that he would neither make war on them nor invade their territory unless they themselves provoked such actions. He also promised not to reinforce Sumter and the Florida post with fighting troops unless the Confederacy attacked them. But, should the two run low on supplies, it would be his duty to provide the men already there with the food needed for survival.

The Sumter men smiled in relief at the President's words. He had made it clear that he wanted a peaceful solution to the North-South crisis. Perhaps, after all, they would be spared trouble. And the promise of food meant that they would not starve, no matter what happened.

The day after entering the White House, Lincoln received a message from Major Anderson saying that Sumter was in desperate need of provisions. The new President ordered a small fleet to be loaded with food for the fort. By April 11, the ships were headed south.

That day, events took a sudden turn at Charleston. A small boat sailed up to Sumter. Out of it stepped several officers sent by Brigadier General Pierre G. T. Beauregard, a Louisiana-born U.S. Army officer who had sided with the South and was now the Confederate commander at

Pierre Gustave Toutant Beauregard earned his place in history by ordering the bombardment of Fort Sumter, thus beginning the Civil War.

Charleston. They told Anderson that Jefferson Davis had learned of the supply ships and believed that Lincoln was committing an act of aggression in dispatching them. They might well be serving as a prelude to an invasion. Consequently, Davis felt that there must be no further delay in commandeering Sumter. It lay in the entryway of a splendid harbor that would be vital to him as a base for receiving supplies in the event of war.

And so, the envoys explained, Davis had wired a message from his capital at Montgomery, Alabama. It ordered Beauregard to demand Sumter's immediate surrender. If Anderson refused to cooperate, the general was to "reduce" the fort to ruins with an artillery bombardment.

Anderson listened quietly and replied that he and his men would "await the first shot." He then said, "If you do not batter the fort to pieces about us, we shall be starved out in a few days."

The envoys returned to Beauregard at Fort Moultrie. Anderson's answer was telegraphed to Davis. Since the Confederacy was no more eager for bloodshed than was the United States, and simply wanted to be allowed to go its own way, Davis asked when Sumter would run out of food. If the fort had to be abandoned before the supply ships arrived, there would be no need for a bombardment that could start a war.

Back to Sumter the envoys went late that night with Davis's question. Anderson's reply: About April 15—unless the supply fleet arrived before then or he received orders from Lincoln to stand his ground. The envoys said that the answer was unacceptable. It left no doubt that the major meant to defend Sumter for as long as possible.

Anderson nodded. He shook hands with the men and, knowing that a bombardment was now inevitable, said, "If we never meet again in this life, I hope that we may meet in the next."

On hearing of Anderson's words, Beauregard ordered the bombardment to begin before dawn on April 12.

The howitzer shell that arced out of Moultrie that morning served as the signal for the start of the bombardment. Forty-three artillery pieces opened fire from their positions around the harbor. They were to continue firing for thirty-six hours, hurling bricks and mortar everywhere, turning the air overhead into a choking cloud of smoke and dust, and creating a thunder that jarred all Charleston awake.

Sumter began to return the fire. The first shot was ordered by Anderson's second-in-command, Captain Abner Doubleday (said by many to have been the inventor of baseball, a claim that is now seriously doubted). It sent a shell screaming out to bounce harmlessly off the iron wall of a small installation. Doubleday continued firing at intervals during the next hours, but his guns were no match for the Confederate artillery. The Sumter troops could do nothing but crouch down, grit their teeth, and hope to survive the rain of incoming shells.

Their anger at being under a brutal attack was joined by frustration later in the day. They shouted happily when Lincoln's supply ships appeared outside the harbor, but then fell silent when the vessels came no closer. Not daring to risk the bombardment, the ships dropped anchor at a safe distance and watched helplessly as the fort was hammered to pieces.

The shelling continued throughout the night. So far, as if by miracle, Anderson's men had been spared one terror. Despite the constant rain of shells, their fort had not caught fire. But, early on April 13, their luck ran out. A bursting shell set a pile of broken wood ablaze. Flames began to spread through the ruins.

When the clouds of smoke from the fire ballooned into the already begrimed sky, Anderson knew that any further defense of Sumter would be useless. So far, as if blessed by another miracle, not one of his men had been killed. Surely, lives would be needlessly lost if he held out any longer.

At that moment, a shell struck the fort's flagstaff. The staff crashed over on its side, carrying the American flag with it. Anderson ordered a soldier to raise a white flag (actually a bed sheet) in the fallen banner's place.

Over at Moultrie, General Beauregard and his troops saw the flash of white in the smoke. They knew that, after 4,000 Confederate shells had been loosed, the siege of Fort Sumter was at an end.

A war that had been brewing for long years and would tear the United States asunder was now at hand.

CHAPTER TWO

On the Road to War

For decades before the first shell burst above Fort Sumter, a jubilant cry could be heard echoing throughout the South: "Cotton is king!"

And indeed it was. From 1800 onward, the South's cotton crop enriched not only the areas where it was grown but also the entire nation. The fiber was purchased by the Northern states and then transformed into cloth products for sale throughout the country. Nations overseas added to the riches by importing tons of the crop for their own use.

Responsible for all the wealth was a clever machine—the cotton gin. Prior to its invention by Eli Whitney in 1793, most Southern farmers had shunned the growing of cotton, concentrating instead on tobacco, sugarcane, and rice. The reason: Cotton had never been a profitable crop. Before it could be sold as a fiber, its seeds had to be pulled from its blooms by hand, a job so arduous that it took a day to remove them from a pound of bloom. Not enough fiber could be produced to turn a decent profit.

The gin changed everything. It could shred the seeds from 50 pounds (23 kilograms) of blooms daily. Suddenly, the farmers who lived in the region that produced the best cotton—a belt that stretched from the Carolinas and Georgia to beyond the Mississippi River—realized that a fortune could now be theirs. Each year, with an army of gins, they could produce tons of the white fiber.

This etching shows Eli Whitney's cotton gin, which had farmers replacing their crops with the more profitable cotton.

Quickly, they replaced their traditional crops with cotton. By 1800, its fluffy blooms were on view in the fields of vast plantations and farms of every size. Cotton was about to become "king."

But it was to bring a terrible problem—the use of black slaves to work the plantations and ready the crop for market.

Slavery

The first black slaves to arrive on American soil—twenty in all—landed in 1619 and were put to work in the Virginia colony. As the thirteen colonies took shape, slaves were

How great a king was cotton in the 1800s? A look at its history tells all.

In 1790, the United States produced approximately 3,000 bales of cotton annually. With a bale weighing about 500 pounds, the entire crop came to around 1.5 million pounds.

But by 1801, the cotton output had jumped to 100,000 bales, for a total of 50 million pounds. From there, it rose to 400,000 bales in 1820, 1.5 million bales in 1840, and an amazing 5.3 million bales in 1860. On the eve of the Civil War, the South was annually producing nearly 90 percent of the world's cotton and bringing in more than $700 million—an amount equaling billions of dollars in today's money.

The South's cotton met all the needs of America's mills, leaving tons available for sale overseas. Great Britain, one of the world's leading manufacturers of cloth, ranked as cotton's best foreign customer. As 1861 dawned, Britain was buying some 90 percent of its cotton from the American South.

shipped into both the North and South. Their total number in the North, where they worked mostly as household servants, stood at approximately 100,000 at the time of the Revolutionary War. By then, the Northern colonies had begun to abolish slavery because it clashed with their democratic ideals and religious principles.

Most slaves were to be found in the agricultural South. Totaling some 300,000 by 1776, they were seen as an economic necessity. They provided an inexpensive labor force for work that required many field hands. A slave could be bought cheaply and then supported for a mere ten cents a day, a fraction of what it would cost to keep a regular hand.

But many Southerners, among them slave-owning George Washington, were uncomfortable with slavery because they thought it immoral. In the wake of the Revolution, they joined such Northerners as Benjamin Franklin and Alexander Hamilton in calling for the practice to be outlawed in the infant country. Consequently, when the Constitution was adopted in 1788, it contained a provision aimed at eventually ending slavery.

The provision held that Congress had the power to ban the practice, but could not use that power until 1808. The long delay marked a compromise between the framers of the Constitution and Georgia and South Carolina. Both states were major rice growers whose farmers claimed that, without slavery, they would never find enough laborers willing to work in their mosquito-infested paddies, where malaria was a constant peril. The two threatened not to sign the Constitution if it endangered slavery, but then agreed to the delay in exchange for other points they wanted to see in the document.

When Congress could finally act in 1808, the legislators outlawed the importation of slaves into the country. They did not, however, ban slavery itself. They allowed the Southerners to continue holding and selling their slaves.

Slavery was allowed to continue within the nation because, by then, the cotton crop was becoming vital to the U.S. economy and was requiring slaves in ever greater numbers to keep pace with the harvests. The Southern planters argued that the end of slavery would do great harm by sending the price of cotton sky-high when they took on the expense of hiring field hands in place of slaves. Congress agreed.

The ban on importation, however, did not stop the flow of slaves into the South. They were now smuggled in aboard ships flying the flags of various nations, among them Great Britain and France (both had recently banned slavery in their own countries). And the traffic increased yearly with the growing need for slaves. By 1820, the slave population had climbed to 1.5 million (in part because of the slave trade, in greater part because of the children born to slave families). In 1860, it stood at approximately 3.5 million.

Free and Slave States

The opposing views of the North and South over slavery were clearly seen in the states that early joined the Union. The Northern additions, among them Vermont in 1791 and Ohio in 1809, entered as "free" states—states that barred slavery. The Southern newcomers, such as Tennessee in 1796 and Louisiana in 1812, were admitted as "slave" states.

Throughout the first half of the 1800s, the slavery issue kept Congress in a turmoil. Trouble loomed whenever a territory asked for admission to the Union, with both the North and South fearing that any newcomer would give the other side a greater degree of political strength. Consequently, Congress was always faced with the problem of keeping the number of slave and free states equal. The legislators met the problem with a series of compromises. Here are three major examples of those actions.

First, in 1820, Congress enacted the Missouri Compromise. It permitted two regions to join the Union at the same time because one, Missouri, was to be a slave state, and the other, Maine, a free state.

The next compromise came at the end of the Mexican War (1846–1848) when Mexico had to surrender two of its major American provinces to the United States—California and New Mexico. The surrender of California led to an 1850 measure that admitted the former province to the Union as a free state to balance slaveholding Texas, which had joined in 1845.

The legislation also divided the New Mexico land into two territories: Utah and New Mexico. The people of each were given the right to vote on whether they wished their region to be free or slave.

This right was known as "popular sovereignty." It came to the forefront again in a third compromise—this time in 1854, after a congressional struggle to decide the future of the vast tract of open land that fanned out from Missouri to the Utah and New Mexico territories. That year, Congress split the area into the territories of Nebraska and Kansas, with popular sovereignty to settle the future of each.

Within two years, the matter of popular sovereignty would lead to bloodshed in Kansas. Paving the way for that tragedy were years of a growing Northern animosity toward slavery.

Years of Fury

From pre-Revolutionary days onward, the Northern dislike of slavery increased until, by the mid-1800s, the system was being widely branded as cruel and criminal (many Northerners, however, gave little thought to the practice, being preoccupied with their own daily lives). The dislike of the practice was shared by a small number of Southerners.

Among the people in both the North and South who most hated slavery were the members of the abolitionist movement. They were deeply committed to seeing it banished everywhere, without regard to the potential harm to the nation's economy. To promote their cause, some of them published newspapers filled with articles describing the cruel treatment meted out to slaves by their masters. Others gave speeches, staged public demonstrations, and flooded Congress with petitions demanding an end to the practice. Still others risked their lives operating the Underground Railroad, a system that secretly moved escaped slaves to freedom in the North.

Though their activities were many, the abolitionists were actually few in number. They nevertheless infuriated the Southern planters and angered the proslavery elements in the North. For the most part in the North, however, they were ignored by the people who gave little thought to slavery and scorned by those who saw them as fanatical troublemakers.

The portrait that the abolitionists painted of slavery was one of brutal mistreatment. In great part, the picture was a true one. The slaves were shipped across the Atlantic in such crowded and filthy conditions that thousands died before reaching their destination. The survivors then had to endure the humiliation of being paraded before buyers at the slave auctions. Later, many were whipped by cruel owners or overseers to make them work harder. Some families were torn apart when an owner sold a mother or a father to a distant plantation.

But there was another side to this dismal picture. Though made to labor long and hard hours, most slaves were not cruelly treated, because most owners were humane people.

The slaves were housed, clothed, and fed by their owners, given the evenings off for their own pleasures, and tended by the owner's doctor when ill. Their young children played with the owner's children. Older slave women cared for the owner's youngsters. In all, most slaves were treated like other servants of the day.

Aside from an owner's sense of humanity, there was a practical reason for avoiding cruel treatment. Between 1800 and 1860, a healthy slave became a very expensive investment, rising from a purchase price of a few dollars to upwards of $1,500. The sensible owner protected the health of this investment. He did not whip a slave for fear of injuring him permanently. Nor did he want to buy a slave whose back was scarred by a whipping. Nor split up a family. Any one of these factors reduced a slave's value as a worker.

Nevertheless, every slave, even those humanely treated, could not escape a cruelty greater than all others—the loss of a lifetime of freedom.

The abolitionists did, indeed, prove to be troublemakers when, in 1854, Congress opted to let popular sovereignty decide the future of the new Kansas and Nebraska territories. Kansas lay south of Nebraska, and its people were expected to vote in favor of its admission to the Union as a slave state. Alarmed at this prospect, the abolitionists sent settlers there in the hope of changing the vote. The South replied with settlers of its own. Kansas was soon the home of two opposing camps, a situation that finally exploded in violence. In 1856, a band of proslavery ruffians attacked the abolitionist town of Lawrence and set it afire. The incident triggered so much fighting between the two factions that the territory soon became known as "Bleeding Kansas."

That fighting led to further trouble. In 1859, John Brown, a wild-eyed abolitionist who had been born in Connecticut and had been active in Kansas, took twenty-one armed men into Virginia. His aim was to incite a massive slave rebellion and put an end to slavery throughout the South once and for all.

On entering the state, Brown attacked the small town of Harpers Ferry. His target there was a small U.S. arsenal that would provide him with guns to arm the slaves for his planned rebellion. He took the installation quickly, but then ran into trouble. He fully expected that hundreds of nearby slaves would rush to his side, but not one arrived. Instead, the townspeople surrounded the arsenal and opened fire. Brown's men were forced to take shelter in a firehouse next door.

There they remained, pinned down, until a contingent of U.S. troops, commanded by Lieutenant Colonel Robert E. Lee, marched into town. Lee offered Brown the chance to surrender. When the offer was refused, the colonel's men stormed the firehouse and, in three minutes, put an end to Brown's grandiose plans.

Over the years, the slavery issue drove such a wedge between the North and South that, by 1860, the United States stood on the threshold of a war with itself.

But there were other wedges also at work. A major problem was the difference in the economies of the North and South. The North was principally an industrial region, while the South was an agricultural area with few industries. This difference led to a number of enduring frictions.

For example, there were disputes over the matter of tariffs—fees charged by the federal government to the nations that shipped goods into the United States. In general, the North wanted high tariffs to protect its manufactured products against the import of inexpensive foreign goods. The South argued for low tariffs—or none whatsoever—so that inexpensive wares from overseas could be traded for cotton. It rankled the Southerners that the Northern mills gobbled up most of the cotton crop and then sold it back to the South in the form of clothing, bedding, tablecloths, and such, all at prices set by the mill owners. Low tariffs could put an end to this practice.

Another factor was the steady growth of Northern might over the years, growth that alarmed the Southerners. The new railroads were unifying the North by connecting its Atlantic ports to areas far to the west. European immigrants were flooding into the North to find work in its factories and mills. In time, the North could become so unified, so heavily populated, and so rich that it would become the nation's dominant region, politically and financially far superior to the South.

Still another problem was the long-standing dispute over the idea of states' rights. At its birth, the United States had established a weak central government, giving the states great powers to decide their own affairs. But as the nation grew, the federal government took on the power to make laws that could supersede those enacted by the individual states. While many people in the North agreed with states' rights, the Southerners were especially protective of the concept. They viewed any federal action against slavery as a violation of those rights.

While the angers generated by slavery and problems such as those above brought the nation to the brink of civil war, it was the election of Abraham Lincoln to the presidency that hurled the country over the precipice. The South greeted his victory with fury. He and his Republican party stood for everything the South hated. They held that slavery was immoral, that Congress should prohibit its further spread into the nation's territories, and that "Bleeding Kansas" should enter the Union as a free state.

Lincoln's victory was too much for South Carolina, Alabama, Florida, Georgia, Louisiana, Mississippi, and Texas. They broke with the Union and formed the Confederate States of America. Their withdrawal was soon followed by what so many Americans had long feared—the outbreak of war when, on April 12, 1861, that first shell streaked in on Fort Sumter from the Charleston shore.

CHAPTER THREE

1861:
First Blood

Before the attack on Sumter, very few people in the North or the South wanted a war and the horror it promised. Myriad Southerners hoped that the Confederate states could be brought peacefully back into the Union. Thousands of Northerners felt that the seceded states should be allowed to stay out of the Union if they so wished and not be forced to return at bayonet point.

But all hopes of avoiding a war vanished with the news from Charleston. Loosed was a series of events that led inexorably to four years of vicious fighting.

First, on April 15, Abraham Lincoln admitted that all hopes for peace had been dashed. It was his task now to preserve a nation—in his words, a "house divided"—that was faced with rebellion. He called for 75,000 volunteers to join the state militias and help quell the uprising.

Overnight, the fall of Sumter had changed the North's sympathetic views toward the Confederacy. They were buried beneath a tidal wave of patriotism. Thousands of men answered Lincoln's call and rushed to join the militias and the regular army. Actually, for many, the idea of abolishing slavery or preserving the Union did not enter into their thinking. They lived in a time when war was still seen as a romantic adventure and that was what they wanted—adventure and the chance to escape the boredom of farm or factory life.

President Abraham Lincoln in 1861, newly elected and determined to preserve the Union.

The President next ordered a naval blockade of the Confederate coasts to intercept the shipments of war materials that the agrarian South could not itself produce and that, along with wares needed by the civilian population, had to be imported in exchange for cotton. The blockade remained on duty throughout the war, intercepting many shipments of needed goods and contributing much to the final collapse of the South.

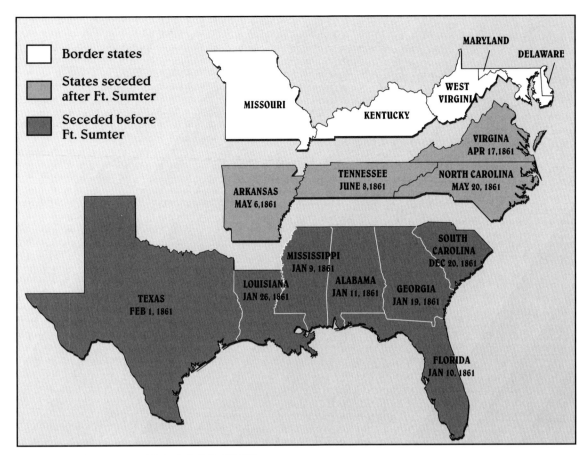

Border states

States seceded after Ft. Sumter

Seceded before Ft. Sumter

MARYLAND

DELAWARE

MISSOURI

WEST VIRGINIA

KENTUCKY

VIRGINIA
APR 17, 1861

ARKANSAS
MAY 6, 1861

TENNESSEE
JUNE 8, 1861

NORTH CAROLINA
MAY 20, 1861

MISSISSIPPI
JAN 9, 1861

SOUTH CAROLINA
DEC 20, 1861

LOUISIANA
JAN 26, 1861

ALABAMA
JAN 11, 1861

GEORGIA
JAN 19, 1861

TEXAS
FEB 1, 1861

FLORIDA
JAN 10, 1861

THE BATTLE LINES ARE DRAWN

Jefferson Davis, on hearing Lincoln's call for 75,000 men, replied in kind. Certain that Lincoln had an invasion in mind, he asked for 100,000 volunteers to bolster the Southern cause. Then, in the next weeks, he saw the Confederacy strengthened by the addition of four states. The newcomers were Virginia, Arkansas, North Carolina, and Tennessee.

These were severe losses for Lincoln. But there was also good news. Four other slave states—Missouri, Kentucky, Maryland, and Delaware—chose to remain with him. Lying adjacent to Union territory and known as the border states, they were vitally important to the President. By staying within the Union, despite the anger of the proslavery supporters in their midst, they reduced the number of enemy bastions right at its doorstep.

The four were later joined by a fifth. When Virginia seceded, the people of its northwestern area refused to cooperate. Independent mountaineers who disliked slavery, they voted to leave Virginia and form a new free state to be called Kanawha. They later changed the name to West Virginia.

A Frightened Washington, D.C.

On Virginia's secession, Jefferson Davis moved to its capital city, Richmond, and began massing troops there. These actions caused deep concern in Washington, D.C., because the two enemy capitals now stood only about 100 miles (160 kilometers) apart. Was Davis planning an attack on Washington?

Many of the city's 61,000 residents feared that a Rebel attack was a certainty. They had good reason to be frightened. Just as a wave of patriotism had flooded through the North after Sumter, so had it washed through the Confederacy. Southerners everywhere had taken up an ominous chant: "On to Washington!"

Further, the city was located just inside Maryland and separated from Virginia only by the Potomac River. It was especially vulnerable to attack. Surely, a gray-uniformed Rebel horde would soon come flooding across the Potomac and overrun the place. The idea so terrified several thousand Washingtonians that they fled in search of safer ground.

Actually, the fears of an invasion were groundless. Davis had no such plan when he began massing troops at Richmond. Rather, he wanted to protect Virginia against a Union assault. Also, Richmond was the center of what little industry the South could boast. Located there were factories capable of producing vital munitions. They had to be safeguarded at all costs.

A Confederate invasion never materialized. But Washington was bristling with some 30,000 militiamen and regular soldiers, and soon a strutting sense of confidence replaced earlier fears. Everyone began demanding a quick defeat of the upstart Rebels.

The demand was picked up and spread nationwide by the press. Though Lincoln felt that the South would likely not be easily defeated, he, too, hoped for a quick victory and ordered an invasion of Virginia with the aim of ending the rebellion in one stroke by capturing Richmond and the Confederate leaders there.

The stage was set for the first major battle of the war.

Death in July

On the hot morning of July 16, 1861, an army of 35,000 U.S. soldiers, now called Federals to differentiate them from the Confederate troops, crossed into Virginia and began to move toward Richmond. Commanded by Brigadier General Irvin McDowell, they presented a handsome sight. In great part, they consisted of state militia units, each sporting its own uniforms. Some were dressed in red and gold, others in gray, and still others in shades of blue.

But the blistering heat soon ruined that fine look. Clouds of dust rose from beneath the marching feet and the wheels of cannons and supply wagons. It settled on uniforms and caked on sweating faces. Many of the soldiers broke ranks and asked for drinks of water at nearby farmhouses. Some dropped to rest beneath trees. Others, looking as if they were on a picnic, stopped to pick blackberries.

Mainly responsible for these lapses in conduct were the militiamen. They were raw recruits who had received just a few weeks of training while camped in Washington. They had yet to become disciplined soldiers.

The marchers moved so slowly that two days passed before they reached Centreville, a town just 27 miles (43 kilometers) from Washington. A short distance ahead was the village of Manassas Junction. It stood beyond Bull Run, a stream that flowed across McDowell's path. Awaiting him on the stream's far side were troops under General Pierre Beauregard of Fort Sumter fame. Some 40 miles (64 kilometers) to the northwest, in the Shenandoah Valley, were additional Rebel troops under Brigadier General Joseph Johnston.

Beauregard, who had been given command of the Confederate army in Virginia, had come to Manassas with 20,000 men and had positioned them along a 10-mile (16-kilometer) stretch of Bull Run. Johnston's troops, numbering 12,000, had gone to the Shenandoah Valley so that they could serve as reinforcements in case Beauregard needed them.

Manassas Junction stood at the southwestern end of Beauregard's 10-mile front. It was here that McDowell planned to strike. But the general rested his men after reaching Centreville—an error because it gave Johnston time to bring some of his reserves down to bolster the Manassas line. Sneaking past a Federal unit that had been sent to keep them from moving to Beauregard's aid, they had done what no military unit in history had ever done. They had come rattling to the battlefront aboard a train.

It was not until Sunday morning, July 21, that McDowell sent his Federals splashing across Bull Run to launch what was to be one of the strangest battles of the Civil War— strange because several thousand civilians had come out from Washington in carriages and on horseback to see what they were sure would be a quick and war-ending Union victory. Cheering, waving flags, and snacking from picnic baskets, they watched the infantry charge the enemy.

The attack stunned the Confederates. They fell back, with McDowell's Federals trailing at a run through a thick wooded area. On reaching open ground, many of the retreating units rallied and began to fight back. But soon the battle developed into an awful pattern for the Rebels. Whenever they stood to fight, they were hurled back by the untrained Union militiamen. Though tasting battle for the first time, the militiamen were performing well in the midst of frightening rifle and cannon fire.

General Thomas "Stonewall" Jackson at the Battle of Bull Run, July 21, 1861.

An especially bad moment for the Rebels came when a Union brigade under Colonel William Tecumseh Sherman drove the troops in front of him back to a spot called Henry House Hill. The Southerners retreated up its sides and across its top, surging past a Virginia contingent led by Brigadier General Thomas Jackson.

As Sherman's troops advanced, Jackson's artillery opened fire and slowed them. The Confederate general then refused to abandon his position—not moving when he was twice wounded nor when eleven cannons were rolled up beneath him and began to batter his position mercilessly. His stubbornness caused an officer to rally some of the retreating Rebels with the shout, "There is Jackson standing like a stone wall!"

The shout won the general the nickname "Stonewall" Jackson. It was to follow him into history.

Elsewhere, the fighting seesawed between the two sides throughout the morning and into the afternoon, but went more and more against the South as the hours passed. By sunset, Beauregard was ready to call off the action so that he could regroup his battered forces and prepare to fight again in the next days.

But before he could do so, help came flooding onto the scene—the rest of Johnston's troops from the Shenandoah Valley. Ready for action, they formed a line and rushed forward. The sight of the oncoming gray uniforms was too much for McDowell's men. Exhausted after hours of fighting, they began to retreat. At first the withdrawal was carried out in good order. The troops left the battlefield and started along a road back to their encampment at Centreville, only to have the raw militiamen, after fighting so well, suddenly reveal how untrained they were.

When Confederate shells began to rain down on them, they panicked and turned the retreat into a terrified flight. Caught up in the mad dash were the civilians who had come out to watch the South's great defeat. Family carriages became trapped in the midst of fleeing soldiers, cannons, and supply wagons. Men, women, and children scattered in terror. Civilians and cavalrymen spurred their horses through open fields. There were screams and gasps as the bursting shells turned the air black with smoke.

When everyone was beyond the reach of Beauregard's cannons, the mad dash slowed to a plodding march. Centreville was forgotten. Washington became everyone's destination. The flight continued through the night. Before dawn, heavy rain began to fall. Morning saw the drenched troops and civilians stagger into the city.

What had been meant to be a glorious victory had ended in a humiliating defeat that cost the lives of 2,900 Union soldiers and 2,000 Confederates.

CHAPTER FOUR

1862:
The Early Fighting

That clash of arms on July 21, 1861, became known by two names. In the North, it was called the Battle of Bull Run and in the South, the Battle of Manassas; the Union designated battles according to nearby bodies of water, while the Confederacy named them for land locations.

Its outcome was greeted with pride in the South and shock in the North, where the people suddenly realized that the rebellion might not be quickly snuffed out. They began to prepare for a long struggle by gearing up their plants for war production. The South did the same with its few factories and arranged for the import of military supplies from overseas.

Lincoln spearheaded the Northern preparations by naming a thirty-five-year-old major general, George B. McClellan, to head the forces stationed at Washington or, as they would soon be called, the Grand Army of the Potomac. The new commander was to whip the untrained men into first-rate fighters and then, because some hope remained for a quick end to the war, march them south for another attempt to capture Richmond.

McClellan was a gifted organizer who did well with the first of these tasks. Daily, he drilled his troops and trained them in battle tactics. The men idolized him and, because of his small size, gave him the affectionate nickname of "Little Mac."

General George B. McClellan was perhaps over-confident at the start of the war, but what really irritated Lincoln was not his confidence but his caution.

In November 1861, Lincoln added to McClellan's duties by naming him commander of all Union forces. But "Little Mac" soon showed a trait that angered Lincoln. He was far too cautious a soldier. A commander must often take risks to win battles, but, fearful of sacrificing his men, McClellan was reluctant to fight unless his army was in perfect order. Consequently, he delayed the Richmond attack throughout the rest of 1861 and the first months of 1862. The delay rankled Lincoln. It gave the South time to train its own men to a fighting pitch.

On virtually all counts, the North and the South were unevenly matched opponents, with the North being the far stronger of the two.

To begin, the North was home to 22 million people, more than twice the South's 9.5 million (of whom some 3.5 million were slaves). According to varying estimates, the Union drew to its ranks between 1.55 and 2.25 million men. The South drew somewhere between 750,000 and 1.08 million.

One of the greatest advantages enjoyed by the North was its industrial might, which produced 92 percent of America's manufactured goods. Housed there were factories, foundries, and machine shops that could be quickly converted to war production. The South, with but few factories, had to import its war materials from overseas.

The South, however, was not without its advantages. One of the most important was the quality of the Confederate officer corps. Wealthy Southerners had long admired military skills and took pride in sending their sons to West Point and then into the army. Some of the finest Southern-born officers, exemplified by Robert E. Lee and Thomas "Stonewall" Jackson, remained loyal to their homeland and provided the troops with an especially talented leadership.

Another advantage was a temporary one. The South at first fielded an army superior to the North's. This was due to the talents of the officer corps and the fact that young Southern men were trained from childhood to handle horses and firearms. These military skills quickly turned them into excellent soldiers. The North, where families were less interested in military prowess, had to depend chiefly on untrained farmers, shopkeepers, and factory workers for its troops. With training and experience, however, the Federal soldiers eventually became the match of the Confederates.

Many Northerners were as irked as the President. They still hoped for a quick end to the war and branded the general with a new and insulting nickname: "Tardy George."

The Civil War was now being waged on two fronts, in the East and to the West. All was quiet on the eastern front, due to McClellan's inaction. And so, Lincoln daily looked westward, out to Missouri.

The War in the West

Though a free state, Missouri was the home of many who sympathized with the South. Among them were men who formed a militia army and set out to topple the state government. In August 1861, they almost achieved their goal when they routed a Federal force sent to crush them. The control of the state hung in the balance until they were finally defeated in March 1862.

Fighting in Missouri was a bearded Union colonel, a West Point graduate who had performed well in the Mexican War. In later years, however, he had damaged his career by falling prey to drink while serving at lonely western outposts and had finally resigned from the army. When the war erupted, he asked to be returned to duty and was appointed to lead militia units being fielded by Illinois. His name was Ulysses S. Grant.

The assignment proved a lucky one for Grant. On leading his new troops into Missouri, he came up against a Rebel militia unit. Knowing they were outnumbered, the Rebels fled and handed him a bloodless victory that won him a promotion to brigadier general and set him on the path to becoming the single greatest Northern leader in the war. He took his first step along that path in late 1861, when he marched his men southeast and captured the Kentucky city of Paducah.

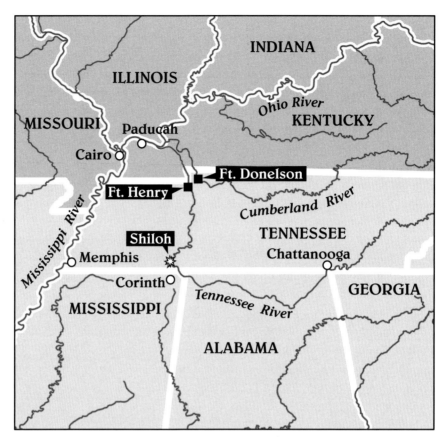

THE CONFEDERATE FORTS HENRY AND DONELSON

The Tennessee Adventure

There was a purpose behind this move. Paducah stood on the Ohio River. Nearby, the Tennessee and Cumberland rivers flowed south out of the Ohio. Together, they moved down into Tennessee. Grant knew that if he could take both he would win a fine advantage for the Union: their use as invasion routes into the Confederacy.

But, like Grant, the Confederate leaders understood the value of the two rivers and had built forts to protect them—the small Fort Henry on the Tennessee and the larger Fort Donelson on the Cumberland. A mere 10 miles (16 kilometers) apart, they were located just inside the Tennessee border.

Grant decided to attack the two with a combined army-navy force. In early February, he sailed along the Tennessee to Fort Henry with 15,000 men and a flotilla of navy gunboats under Commodore Andrew Foote. On reaching the fort, he ordered the gunboats to open fire, only to have its commander quickly surrender. Thinking the fort indefensible, the commander had sent most of his men to Fort Donelson.

The delighted Grant now moved overland to Donelson while Foote hurried back to the Ohio River, sailed to the Cumberland, and swept up to Donelson on February 14. There, he made a mistake. He probed too close before opening his bombardment. The heavily defended fort returned fire, putting two of his gunboats out of action, wounding the commodore, and forcing him to withdraw a few miles upriver.

When Grant reached Donelson, he saw the damage being inflicted on Foote. Realizing that a direct attack would cost too many men, he formed an arc around the fort and began to lay siege to the installation with his artillery.

The troops at Fort Donelson knew that a siege could starve them into surrender. On February 15, they burst out through the front gate and hit the right side of Grant's line with an attack meant to lead them to freedom. At first, the action almost succeeded. Flinging the enemy back, the Confederates carved a narrow opening in the Union line.

Grant was several miles away at the time, visiting the wounded Foote. He galloped back to his line, rallied his soldiers, and sent them rushing to reinforce their beleaguered comrades. In fierce fighting, they closed the escape route and drove the Confederates back inside the fort.

That night, Grant received a note from General Simon Bolivar Buckner, the fort's commander. In it, Buckner asked what terms Grant would require for a surrender. Grant wrote a terse reply that left Buckner with no choice but to abandon the post or face starvation. The reply: "No terms except an unconditional and immediate surrender...."

Fort Donelson passed into Grant's hands on February 16. The word of his victory spread through the North and transformed him into a national hero, a fighting general who was the exact opposite of the cautious McClellan. In particular, his reply to Buckner delighted everyone. He was quickly dubbed "Unconditional Surrender" Grant. A pleased Lincoln promoted him to the rank of major general.

McClellan at Richmond

In March 1862, a month after Grant's victory, McClellan launched his long-awaited invasion of Virginia. He did so not of his own accord but because of two actions by the impatient Lincoln. First, the President relieved him of the command of all the Union forces so that he could concentrate fully on the invasion. Second, Lincoln ordered him to move.

Known as the Peninsular Campaign, the invasion began when a fleet of Union gunboats and 400 transports carried some 112,000 men down the Potomac River to Chesapeake Bay and then farther south to the York Peninsula on the southeastern coast of Virginia. When McClellan put his troops ashore in early April, Richmond lay just 60 miles (96 kilometers) away. His plan was to strike the capital through its side door.

The peninsula was bordered on its sides by the York and James rivers. McClellan intended to advance up the peninsula with gunboats moving along the rivers and protecting his flanks. But he immediately ran into a problem that kept the warships from accompanying him. The York shoreline was heavily planted with Confederate artillery, while the James was safeguarded by the ironclad warship *Merrimack*, which single-handedly could stop all his wooden gunboats.

Worse, he had fewer men than he had anticipated when planning his campaign, because a small Confederate army under General Stonewall Jackson was operat-

Although the French and British had been experimenting with them since the late 1850s, ironclad warships were first used in battle during the American Civil War.

The most historic meeting of ironclads occurred in March 1862, after an armor-plated ship attacked a trio of Lincoln's blockading vessels at Hampton Roads, Virginia. The ship had once been a Union frigate called the *Merrimack* (sometimes spelled *Merrimac*). Scuttled by Federal sailors when the Confederacy took over Hampton Roads at the start of the war, it had been raised and turned into a low-lying vessel armed with ten guns and sheathed in iron plating.

As a wooden ship goes down in flames beside them, the ironclad *Monitor* and *Merrimack* ships battle in the harbor.

(continued)

Rechristened the *Virginia*, but still usually called by its original name, the ironclad attacked the three blockaders on the afternoon of March 8. It sank one and forced another to strike its colors, surrendering. Then, planning to sink the third blockader on the following day, the *Merrimack* returned to port.

That night, however, a new Union ironclad appeared on the scene. Carrying two cannons inside a revolving turret, it had just been completed at a Brooklyn shipyard and had been sent to help fight the *Merrimack*.

Early on the morning of March 9, the *Merrimack* sailed out for its final kill and found itself facing the newcomer, the *Monitor*. The two ironclads traded fire, with neither sinking the other. At last, low on powder and leaking, the *Merrimack* withdrew. Other than standing off York Peninsula during the Peninsular Campaign, the ship played no further role in the war.

That battle on March 9, 1862, changed naval history. It marked the passing of the wooden warship and the emergence of the first of the modern naval vessels.

The Union built a number of ironclad gunboats that would eventually assist in the successful campaigns to wrest control of the Mississippi River from the Confederacy.

ing in northern Virginia's Shenandoah Valley. Jackson was attacking Union communications lines, successfully skirmishing with Federal units, capturing arms and ammunition, and filling Washington with the fear that he would attack the capital as soon as the Army of the Potomac departed for York Peninsula. As a result, Lincoln had ordered McClellan to leave 35,000 troops behind to protect the city.

Feeling undermanned, the general now reluctantly set out along the peninsula. He moved toward his first target, a Confederate line of 15,000 men that stretched clear across his path. They had been placed there by General

Joseph Johnston of the Bull Run campaign. He was now commanding the Rebel troops in Virginia.

McClellan, on the basis of faulty army intelligence, thought that the line was manned by troops equal in strength to his. Cautious as ever, he did not attack but decided to weaken the defenders with a month-long artillery siege.

When he finally struck in May, he found that most of their number had quietly moved back to Richmond. The remaining units, though fighting valiantly, were outgunned and had to give way, enabling him to overrun two small cities—Yorktown, the site of the British surrender in the Revolutionary War, and nearby Williamsburg.

From Williamsburg, McClellan slogged on to Richmond and finally camped a few miles outside the city in mid-May. Again he delayed attacking, this time for two reasons. First, Union intelligence said the city was defended by a force twice the size of his. (As before, the information was dead wrong; his Federals actually outnumbered the Rebels at least 100,000 to 60,000.)

Second, Stonewall Jackson was raising more havoc up in the Shenandoah Valley and, before the month was out, would drive one Union force back across the Potomac to Washington, rekindling the fears there that he was about to invade the city. Thanks to Stonewall's heroics, Lincoln was refusing McClellan's requests for the additional troops that the general felt were needed for the assault on Richmond.

And so McClellan sat where he was, and it was Johnston who attacked. On May 31, he hit the Union line at a point 9 miles (14 kilometers) outside Richmond.

The battle, known as Seven Pines–Fair Oaks because it was fought near a railroad station called Seven Pines and the farm Fair Oaks, raged for two days. It ended with Johnston's troops retreating to Richmond, and cost him 5,700 casualties as opposed to 4,400 for McClellan. Johnston himself was wounded and hospitalized.

With Johnston now unable to lead the Richmond force, command went to the former colonel who had defeated

John Brown at Harpers Ferry, the gentlemanly Major General Robert E. Lee. At the onset of the war, he had been offered the command of all Union troops, but had chosen to remain loyal to his home state of Virginia. He had since served as a military adviser to Jefferson Davis. Now he was destined to be the South's greatest military figure.

On taking command, Lee gave the Richmond force the name by which it would be known throughout the war—the Army of Northern Virginia—and decided on an all-out thrust against McClellan. On June 26, he threw his entire army against McClellan.

The Seven Days' Battle

The period of fighting known as the Seven Days' Battle saw the two sides clash at a series of rural locations, among them Mechanicsville and Gaines Mill. In terms of men lost, each meeting was a Rebel defeat. For example, at Gaines Mill, Lee suffered 8,750 casualties to 4,000 for McClellan. But they were actually victories, because McClellan retreated to form new defensive lines after each encounter.

The Seven Days' Battle reached its climax on July 1 at a spot called Malvern Hill. Here, along the hillside and atop its 150-foot (46-meter) peak, McClellan massed his troops in his best defensive position to date. When Lee saw the Union lines, he thought them impenetrable and wondered if he should turn back to Richmond. But he remembered "Little Mac's" habit of retreating. Perhaps he would repeat himself again. Lee decided to gamble.

The gamble led to a massacre. More than 100 cannons were mounted on Malvern Hill. They answered Lee's opening bombardment with a return fire that knocked out his gun positions one by one. Then they joined the infantry in focusing on the waves of Confederates who advanced stubbornly toward the hillside. Cannon and rifle fire tore the oncomers to pieces in the next hours. The bloodshed finally ended when a shaken Lee ordered a retreat after 5,500 of his soldiers had lost their lives.

McClellan, with his usual caution, did not pursue Lee. Rather, he rested his men, plotted his next move against Richmond, and asked Lincoln to send him additional troops so that he would have the strength to take the city. The second attempt to capture the Confederate capital had failed. Would it ever, Lincoln wondered, fall into Union hands?

CHAPTER FIVE

1862: Grant and Farragut on the Western Front

As the North and South were watching McClellan at Richmond, they were also looking west. There, two major Union campaigns were in progress—one led by Ulysses S. Grant and the other by the Navy's Captain David G. Farragut.

Grant on the Move

In March, soon after the surrender of Fort Donelson, Grant moved south through Tennessee while Commodore Foote's gunboats sailed back to the Ohio River and on to the Mississippi for action there. Grant's target was Corinth, Mississippi, a short distance beyond the Tennessee border. The city was rapidly becoming a stronghold to bar any further Union advance into the Confederacy. Massing there under the command of Lieutenant General Albert S. Johnston (no relation to General Johnston at Richmond) was an army that would soon number 44,000 men.

Working with Johnston was General Beauregard, who had come west after Bull Run. The two officers were now awaiting not only Grant but also an army led by Major General Don Carlos Buell. Buell had swept into Tennessee from the north and had captured the city of Nashville in late February. At present, he was moving toward Corinth in Grant's wake and was due to overtake him at the Tennessee River near the Mississippi border. Together, the two armies totaled 60,000 troops.

With Buell close behind, Grant arrived at the river in early April. He sent his men over to Pittsburg Landing on the far side, where they fanned out and moved inland for about 2 miles (3 kilometers). Buell's troops finally stopped and made camp some 10 miles (16 kilometers) to Grant's rear.

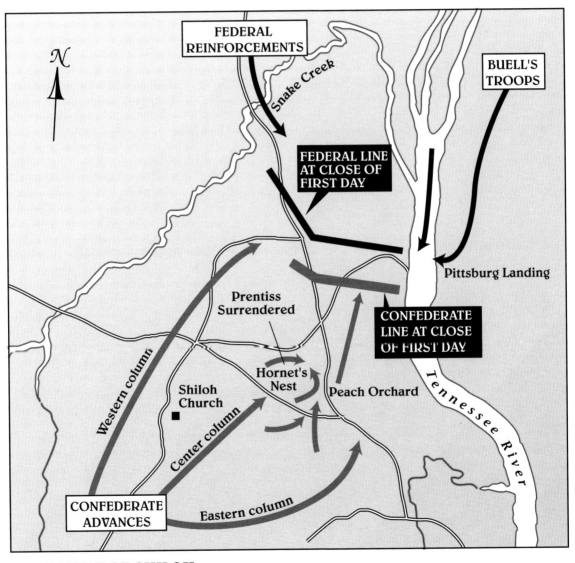

THE BATTLE OF SHILOH

Grant felt certain that Johnston would not attack him at Pittsburg Landing but would wait for the Union troops to throw themselves against fortress Corinth. After Fort Donelson, the Union general had been given additional troops, most of whom were raw recruits, and he thought it safe to spend several days training them for the assault on Corinth. But Johnston, though solidly fortified, was in no mood to fight a defensive war. Determined to drive the Federals back across the Tennessee River, he hit them with a surprise attack early on April 6, triggering the two-day bloodbath that was to be remembered simply as Shiloh.

Two Days of Death

Johnston divided his army into three columns that drove north toward Pittsburg Landing in parallel thrusts. The center column struck first at a Union camp 2 miles from the Landing. The Federals there fought back for a time, but were finally forced to retreat, falling back with their commander, Brigadier General Benjamin Prentiss, to a road running between two earthen walls about 2 feet (.6 meter) deep. Rallying and using the road as a ready-made trench, they began to return the Rebel fire. Numbering more than 1,000 troops, they were to hold the Rebels at bay for hours to come. Their "trench" was soon christened the Hornets' Nest.

A short distance away, the western column swept in on the small Methodist meetinghouse that was to give the battle its name—Shiloh Church—and that was now serving as the headquarters for Brigadier General William T. Sherman of the Bull Run campaign. His men were raw recruits. Terrified by the din of battle, they fled into the surrounding woods, with some of them hiding in the underbrush or in caves for the day.

But Sherman galloped after the troops and managed to regroup many of their number. Under his leadership, they spent the next hours savagely resisting the oncoming gray tide—but always in vain. Relentlessly, the Confederates pushed them back toward Pittsburg Landing.

This etching is of the terrible Battle of Shiloh, with the Shiloh Chapel in the background.

A little distance from the Hornets' Nest, the attack's eastern column ran into trouble when it entered a peach orchard and was checked all morning long by enemy artillery and rifle fire. When General Johnston rode up to assess their situation, he saw that a stretch of open ground lay to their right and was overlooked by a Union-held hill. He ordered that the hill be taken and then, on horseback, led the charge himself. Defying a withering fire, his men dashed across the open space, reached the hill, and mounted its slopes. Moments later, their bayonets drove the Federals off the summit.

As Johnston rode up the hillside, his uniform was ripped by rifle fire and a hot pain knifed through one leg.

Despite the pain, he ignored the wound. He remained in the saddle, shouting orders to his men, only to feel himself growing weak. The color drained from his face.

Two aides, seeing that he was wounded, helped him dismount and placed him in a spot protected from the enemy fire. As the fifty-nine-year-old general lay there with blood seeping through his boot, the life drained out of him. He died at 2:30 P.M. of a minié ball that had pierced an artery.

With Johnston's death, his command passed to Beauregard. Beauregard brought sixty-two artillery pieces forward to batter the Union retreat all along the battlefront. Beyond the hill where Johnston had died, the Confederates steadily drove on toward Pittsburg Landing. Some of their number swung left to plunge in behind Prentiss, who was still holding on at the Hornets' Nest. Surrounded, he finally surrendered at 5:30 in the afternoon.

By then, the Confederates were pressing in on Pittsburg Landing from two sides. On the south side, the eastern column came within sight of its docks, but was stopped by a contingent of General Buell's troops that had come up from their reserve positions. A mile or so to the north, the western column was battling along a defensive line that Grant had established.

At 6:00 P.M., Beauregard ordered his troops to cease firing. There was no use fighting in the coming darkness. His men were exhausted and almost out of ammunition. He would have to resupply them and resume the battle in the morning.

Beauregard was to regret the necessary cease-fire order. Grant spent the night preparing for an attack of his own. He brought two divisions of Buell's army forward to Pittsburg Landing. Also arriving was a force under Brigadier General Lew Wallace that had been guarding supplies some miles to the north. Rounding out the Union troops were the many men who had regained their courage after a day in hiding.

The attack came at dawn. It was now the Confederates' turn to retreat. The pursuing Federals cascaded down the hillside where Johnston had died. They crashed through the peach orchard. They raced past the Hornets' Nest. Finally, they pressed in on little Shiloh Church.

There, the artillery of both sides shattered trees and threw up geysers of earth. Soldiers fired at each other from behind trees and rocks. The ground became littered with the bodies of the dead and wounded. Some of the dead were locked together as they had been at the moment of death while fighting hand-to-hand.

The battle raged for hours, with the tide always running in the Union's favor. At last, at 2:30 P.M., Beauregard realized the futility of fighting on and ordered a retreat. Exhausted, the Confederates reeled back toward the safety of Corinth. Grant did not send his troops in pursuit. They were as spent as the Rebels. He ordered them to rest.

And so it was that one of the bloodiest battles in the Civil War came to an end. Close to 25,000 men lost their lives or were wounded in the grassy and wooded land that lay between Pittsburg Landing and Shiloh Church—13,700 for the Union, and 10,700 for the Confederacy.

Though the battle was technically a draw, it was actually a Union victory because a greatly reduced Confederate force returned to Corinth. But it was a personal defeat for Grant. His troops were serving with the Union Army of the West, which was commanded by Major General Henry Halleck. Halleck had long been jealous of his subordinate's battlefield abilities and now took over Grant's forces so that he could claim the glory for taking Corinth. Grant served as his second-in-command but was pushed aside as Halleck spent the next days building his troop strength for the Corinth attack. Then he began a snail-like move on the city, advancing as little as one mile a day, much to Grant's disgust.

In Corinth, Beauregard watched Halleck's approach. Knowing he was far outnumbered, and with his men riddled with dysentery, he finally decided to abandon the small city and save his soldiers for future action. When Halleck finally arrived on May 30, he was able to take Corinth without a fight.

Fortunately for Grant, Halleck did not remain on the scene for long but was summoned to Washington by Lincoln and given a new assignment. Grant again took command of the troops and began plotting his next move—a march south to help wrest the city of Vicksburg, Mississippi, from Confederate hands.

Farragut at New Orleans

Some ten days after Johnston launched his attack on Pittsburg Landing, a fleet of more than forty steam-powered Union warships entered the Mississippi River from the Gulf of Mexico. They were commanded by sixty-year-old Captain David G. Farragut. His orders from Washington were simple: Sail up the river and take the city of New Orleans.

Both the Mississippi and New Orleans were vital to the Confederacy. The river served as a roadway for the movement of goods, munitions, and troops, and as a crossover to the heart of the Confederacy for wares—especially cattle from Texas—that arrived from the West.

New Orleans, located some 110 miles (177 kilometers) from the Gulf, was the Confederacy's leading port. It received war supplies and food from the ships that successfully ran Lincoln's naval blockade. Conversely, it served as a main port of departure for Southern goods to the outside world. If the city could be taken, the Confederacy would suffer a terrible blow and the Mississippi would be open to further Union probes along its length.

Because of the city's importance, the river roadway to it was strongly defended. Some 75 miles (120 kilometers) below the city, the Mississippi was guarded by two forts: St. Philip on the east bank and Jackson on the west shore.

Together, they boasted 126 artillery pieces and 1,200 men. A fleet of warships hovered just upriver of the two.

It was this array of defensive might that Farragut encountered when he reached the forts on April 18 and ordered his leading ships to open fire. For almost a week, his sweating crews unleashed 250 shells an hour at their targets. The forts, joined by the warships from upriver, returned the fire but did minimal damage, because Farragut kept his ships constantly shifting about to avoid becoming easy targets.

By the fifth day of the artillery duel, Farragut was growing impatient. Too much time was being taken to level the forts. To break the deadlock, he elected to sail past them and hurry on to New Orleans. It was a dangerous strategy because it would bring him directly under their guns, but he felt it was worth the risk. He was confident that once he took New Orleans, the commander of the forts would surrender, realizing that further fighting was useless.

At 2:00 A.M. on April 24, Farragut moved north with the hope of slipping past under the cover of darkness. But he was sighted. Shells began to crash down on him from both shorelines. Enemy gunboats came rushing at him. Two rammed one of his ships and sent it to the bottom. But he steadily inched forward, finally putting the danger behind him and facing a clear run to New Orleans.

At word of Farragut's approach, the military commander at the city withdrew his 3,000-man force to avoid capture. He took along as many military supplies as possible. Before leaving, his troops set fire to the warehouses containing all the stores that had to be left behind. Hundreds of citizens joined the effort to keep anything of value from falling into Farragut's hands. They poured barrels of molasses into the streets, dumped bales of cotton into the river, and set fire to two warships under construction at dockside.

Farragut sailed up to the defenseless New Orleans under rolling clouds of smoke and took possession of the city on April 25. There word reached him that, as he had guessed, the two forts downriver had surrendered once he had passed them.

With New Orleans captured, Farragut moved on to Vicksburg, Mississippi, but turned away when he realized that his ships could not take the city because of its heavy defenses. To the north, at the point where Kentucky, Tennessee, and Missouri met the Mississippi, Commodore Foote's gunboats, reinforced by army troops, had earlier captured the heavily defended river post known as Island Number 10. In the next months, naval forces maneuvered down the river until only Vicksburg and its surrounding area remained under Confederate control.

Grant arrived in the Vicksburg area during the winter. It was there that, in 1863, he would win his next great victory.

1862: Lee and McClellan on the Eastern Front

By June 1862, Abraham Lincoln was again disgusted with McClellan. "Tardy George," after drawing close to Richmond and battering Joseph Johnston at Seven Pines–Fair Oaks, was still sitting outside the city (with the Seven Days' Battle yet to come). Something had to be done to put life into the war on the eastern front.

The President's solution was to bring in Major General John Pope from Halleck's western army and give him command of the troops at Washington. Next, he named Halleck to head all the Union forces. Finally, soon after the Seven Days' Battle, he recalled McClellan to Washington and assigned his troops to Pope, a humiliating demotion for "Tardy George."

Lincoln felt certain he would get action from Pope. The general had won his new job because of the help he had given Foote in capturing the heavily defended Island 10 on the Mississippi River. But Pope soon proved himself a boastful officer whose actions did not measure up to his words when he met Robert E. Lee in battle. As a result of that meeting, Pope's command of his army came to an end almost as soon as it had begun.

The Second Battle of Bull Run

At the time of Pope's appointment, his troops were entrenched near Bull Run, poised to stop any attack that

General Robert E. Lee and his horse, Traveler.

Lee might launch at Washington. Lee, however, had no intention of attacking. With McClellan at Richmond's doorstep, he could not spare the troops. Further, after Malvern Hill, he needed time to rebuild his tattered army.

But then, in August, the Peninsular Campaign ended with McClellan's recall to Washington. Suddenly, Richmond was no longer threatened. Here was a golden opportunity to drive Pope out of Virginia.

This Lee did by marching his Army of Northern Virginia, which consisted of 30,000 men under Lieutenant General James Longstreet and 25,000 commanded by Stonewall Jackson, to Bull Run. There, he sent the lanky Jackson curling around Pope's right flank to attack from behind while Longstreet shredded the enemy's left flank. The battle—called Second Bull Run by the Union and Second Manassas by the South—raged through August 29 and 30, drove virtually all the Union troops out of northern Virginia, and cost Pope his job. Not knowing what else to do, Lincoln handed Pope's command back to George McClellan.

Into Union Territory

The victory at Bull Run presented Lee with another opportunity. The Federal retreat had left the way into the Union completely open to him. He had his first chance to invade the North.

It was a heady but dangerous idea. His troops had paid a terrible price in the Seven Days' Battle—20,000 dead and wounded. They were exhausted. Their uniforms were in tatters. They were low on food and ammunition. Could they now handle a thrust deep into enemy territory?

For Lee, the answer had to be "yes." He must seize this new opportunity, and seize it before the Federals could regroup and fight back. He sent a message to Jefferson Davis, asking for permission to invade Maryland and then Pennsylvania. Davis's consent was quickly given.

In addition to wanting to stagger the North with a demoralizing blow, Lee and Davis held a secret hope for the invasion. Several European nations, among them Great Britain and France, were quietly hoping for the war to end with a Confederate victory. Such a victory would give them the advantage of dealing with two economically weak countries rather than a single American giant.

Both men knew that Britain and France were thinking of proposing a peace plan that was based on granting independence to the Confederacy. A successful invasion of the North might prod them into presenting it. If so, the Union would surely be infuriated and reject the idea, an action that could prompt Britain and France to intervene in the fighting on the South's side. It was this possibility that made Lee and Davis willing to risk the invasion.

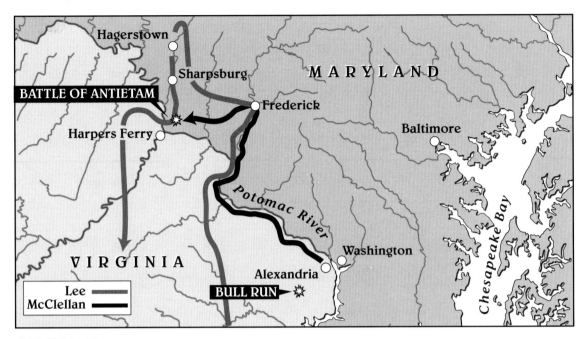

ANTIETAM

And so, on September 4, a week after Bull Run, Jackson and Longstreet took their troops into Maryland. Many of the men thought they were heading for Washington and were startled when they swung wide of the city and marched north to the town of Frederick. The fact was that Lee had never intended to attack the capital. He planned instead to disrupt the communications between the Union's eastern and western fronts by cutting telegraph lines and railroad tracks—a job that his men did quite well—and then advance from Frederick to Hagerstown and on into Pennsylvania.

In Washington, when the reappointed McClellan learned of the invasion, he once again showed his great organizational skills. He swiftly equipped the Bull Run survivors and inspired all his soldiers, 90,000 strong, to meet their next task—the expulsion of the Rebel upstarts. Then he led them in pursuit of Lee, tracking him to Frederick and on toward Hagerstown.

He overtook the enemy's rearguard units near the town of Sharpsburg, 15 miles (24 kilometers) south of Hagerstown. They fought a delaying action to slow McClellan's progress, at the same time sending word to Lee that the Federals were snapping at his heels. Lee was already in Hagerstown when the warning arrived. He rushed back to Sharpsburg and established a line of defense there.

The line took shape between two waterways. Flowing behind it was a stretch of the Potomac River. Between one and two miles to its front was a peaceful stream called Antietam Creek. It would give the North its name for what would be the bloodiest single-day battle of the war. The South would remember the day's fighting as Sharpsburg.

The Single Worst Day

McClellan reached Antietam Creek on September 15. In the distance, across an area of woods, pastures, and fields of grain, he could see the Confederate line. It extended in two directions from Sharpsburg, with Jackson's entrenchments spearing northward, and Longstreet's southward. Though the Confederates were still readying their defenses, McClellan did not attack. Cautious as always, he rested his men for two days while bringing up supplies for the coming battle. That extra time allowed Lee the opportunity to strengthen his positions.

McClellan opened the battle with a move against Jackson's line at sunrise on September 17. The attack took the Federals through a cornfield, only to be thrown back across it when they reached the far side. They regrouped and attacked again. Again, they were repulsed and, again, they attacked. In the next hours, the cornfield repeatedly changed hands. Its stalks, head-high at dawn, were leveled by gunfire. The ground became so littered with the fallen men of both sides that a soldier later said it was possible to cross the field without ever touching the ground.

This photo was taken after the Battle of Antietam. Even hardened army officials were shocked by the number of dead and wounded.

At mid-morning, with Jackson's men holding their line, the battle shifted a bit south to a point close to Sharpsburg. Here, the Federals came to a lane running between two high banks and met massed Confederate fire. The struggle for the pathway, which the Federals soon nicknamed "Bloody Lane," lasted until 1:00 P.M. When they finally plunged down its banks, they found it piled high with the dead and wounded. Nearby, a dead Rebel soldier lay across a fence. His body was riddled with more than fifty bullets.

Clara Barton, founder of the Red Cross

Millions of women played a vital role in the Civil War. They not only maintained the homes but carried on the fieldwork that their men had left behind. In addition, they sewed clothing and prepared gift parcels for the absent men, visited the patients in military hospitals, and raised funds to help support the war.

(continued)

Further, in a time when women were thought incapable of working outside the home, thousands proved otherwise. They successfully held down jobs in factories, mills, and government offices, thus freeing men for the fighting.

Women, however, performed their greatest service in the war's hospitals. Professional and volunteer nurses tended the Union and Confederate wounded throughout the war years. Coming from all walks of life, they included in their ranks such well-remembered figures as Clara Barton, who later formed the American Red Cross; a young Louisa May Alcott, yet to win fame as the author of *Little Women*; and former slave Harriet Tubman, who helped escaped slaves reach the North via the Underground Railroad in the prewar years.

One of the most influential women of the Civil War era did not serve in any capacity during the fighting. She was Harriet Beecher Stowe, the abolitionist writer who, in the early 1850s, published the internationally popular novel *Uncle Tom's Cabin*. Reflecting her life-long hatred of slavery in its depiction of slave life in the South, the book greatly stimulated the growth of the abolitionist movement and brought the American slavery issue to worldwide attention.

As "Bloody Lane" was being assaulted, McClellan threw an attack against Longstreet south of Sharpsburg. To reach the enemy, the Federals had to cross a small bridge spanning Antietam Creek. They were repulsed three times by artillery and rifle fire before making their way to the far side. From there, they struggled forward and, by 4:00 P.M., seemed about to shatter Longstreet's line.

Longstreet was saved when new troops rushed onto the scene. During Lee's northward move, they had been sent over to Harpers Ferry (in the Virginia region that had remained with the Union and would soon be called West Virginia) to clear the area of any Federals who might be there. Now, though bone-weary at the end of a fast-paced march of 17 miles (27 kilometers), they managed to turn back the Federal thrust in the waning hours of the afternoon. Sunset brought an end to the day's fighting, with the Confederate lines, though battered, still intact.

There was not to be another day of battle. Exhausted, both Lee and McClellan remained in place throughout September 18. Then Lee, having suffered 13,700 casualties, moved back into Virginia, his dream of invading the North shattered—at least for the time being.

McClellan, with 12,350 casualties but with a force that still far outnumbered that of his opponent, once again let his cautious nature take over. He did not pursue Lee's beaten troops and overpower them in a battle that might have ended—or at least shortened—the war. Lincoln threw up his hands for the last time and removed him from command. "Little Mac," considered a fine soldier by officers on both sides despite his caution, retired and did not fight again in the war.

Though Antietam brought an end to McClellan's career, the battle was clearly a Union victory. It had thwarted Lee's plans for the North. Each side had lost approximately the same number of men, but the percentage of Lee's losses was greater because his army was the smaller of the two. Finally, the show of strength by the Union forces kept Britain and France from intervening in the war on the side of the South. They decided that the North was bound to win in the end.

On dismissing McClellan, Lincoln was faced with the task of choosing a replacement to lead the Army of the Potomac. He selected Major General Ambrose Burnside, who had fought at Antietam. The appointment was to prove a disastrous one.

The Year's Last Fighting

Three major engagements were to follow Antietam and end the fighting of 1862. First, despite the tragedy at Antietam, the Confederacy attempted another invasion of the North in early October when General Braxton Bragg marched out of Chattanooga, Tennessee, and headed for Ohio. He never reached his destination, but was stopped at Perryville, Kentucky, and fell back to Tennessee, where his troops settled in at the town of Murfreesboro.

Next, in November, General Burnside led 100,000 men into Virginia for the fourth Union strike at Richmond. Burnside was a modest man who felt that he was not blessed with great military skills. This self-assessment proved accurate when his troops reached the town of Fredericksburg in mid-December.

It was there that the exhausted Lee, on hearing of the approaching Burnside, stationed 62,000 troops to intercept him. The two forces clashed on December 13 and 14, with Burnside fighting his way through the town and then coming up to a 1,200-foot (365-meter) -long stone wall behind which the Confederates were massed. He rashly ordered a series of frontal attacks, only to be hurled back each time by nonstop rifle fire. At last, after having suffered 12,700 casualties (with some 6,000 dead), Burnside withdrew to Washington in disgrace.

The year's final battle took place on the western front. When Braxton Bragg's Confederates retreated from Perryville to Murfreesboro, they became the targets of a year-end Union attack. It was launched on December 31, and the battle raged for three days. The air was so filled with the roar of artillery fire that the men in a Rebel unit once stopped in a cotton field to stuff their ears with cotton blooms. The battle cost each side 12,000 casualties and ended in a draw, after which both went into winter quarters to ready themselves for the new year's fighting.

CHAPTER SEVEN

1863: Warring West and East— Vicksburg and Chancellorsville

The year 1863 did not open with a major military campaign. Instead, Abraham Lincoln began the year with the announcement of a document he had spent months preparing: the Emancipation Proclamation.

In it, he declared that certain slaves were henceforth to be "forever free."

The Emancipation Proclamation

Throughout 1861 and 1862, the President avoided saying that he was waging war to free the nation's slaves. Rather, he claimed to be fighting to preserve the Union, hoping that his words would placate the Confederate states and make it easier for them to abandon the war one day and rejoin the Union. He also hoped to please the slaveholding border states and thus keep them within the Union. (Neither side openly admitted that the war was being fought over slavery; the South contended that it was fighting not to hold on to its slaves but to protect its states' rights.)

Lincoln's stance worried his advisers. They daily reminded him that the antislavery factions in the North were clamoring for the abolition of the practice. If he ignored their demand, he would weaken, or even end, their support of the war. Agreeing, Lincoln began preparing the Emancipation Proclamation in 1862. But he delayed making it public because of the failures to capture Richmond.

The President believed that until the Union showed some genuine military strength, the Proclamation would cause people to suspect he was confessing that he could not subdue the South. They would think he was hoping that the freed slaves would rise and do the job for him.

Such suspicions would be disastrous. At home, they would discourage the Northerners from continuing the war. Abroad, they could cause Britain and France to join the fighting on the side of the South.

The delay came to an end with Lee's failed invasion of the North. Because of the Union's show of strength at Antietam, Lincoln knew that he could now safely issue the Proclamation. He did so on January 1, 1863.

The Proclamation has long been one of the most misunderstood documents in U.S. history. Many Americans think that it freed every slave in the nation. It did not. Instead, it declared that only the slaves in the states rebelling against the Union were to be "forever free." It avoided mention of the slaves in the border states in order to keep those states from abandoning the Union. Nor did it mention those in areas of the Confederacy that had come under Union control.

In all, with the Confederate states ignoring it, the Proclamation did not free a single slave. Rather, it set the stage for slaves to be freed in any Rebel state that later fell to the Union. Further, it left little doubt that the war was indeed being fought over slavery, a fact that caused anger among the many Federals who were willing to risk their lives to preserve the Union but not for the liberation of black slaves.

Finally, along with the Antietam victory, it kept Britain and France out of the war. Now that slavery was an open issue, they dared not fight alongside the South. They would

In 1862, the Union army began admitting a few black troops to its ranks. The enlistments grew in the next years and, by the war's close, some 200,000 black men, all eager to join in a conflict that promised to end slavery, had seen service, with 37,000 sacrificing their lives.

At first, the troops faced a problem—the widespread white feeling that black men would never make courageous fighters. They proved this to be a prejudiced and empty view when units such as the 54th Massachusetts Regiment performed gallantly in battle.

When, in 1863, a Union force landed on Morris Island in the harbor of Charleston, South Carolina, the men of the 54th spearheaded the attack against the fort there. They reached the parapets before being repulsed, only to strike again and again until a heavy bombardment by the guns at nearby Fort Sumter forced them into a final withdrawal. Several days later, the Confederates abandoned the island.

Of the 600 black men in the battle, 250 lost their lives. For his bravery in the fighting, Sergeant William H. Carney became the first black soldier to be awarded the Congressional Medal of Honor. Thirty-seven black Americans were to win the nation's highest decoration before the war's end.

Other black units performed as magnificently as the 54th. Among them were the 55th Massachusetts Regiment, the 11th U.S. Colored Troops, and seven cavalry units. A total of thirty-seven black regiments participated in the Virginia fighting that brought the war to a close in 1865.

Toward the end of the war, the Confederacy considered enlisting blacks but rejected the idea on the grounds that their enlistment would demoralize the Southern white troops. The idea was accepted later, but the Confederacy fell before the black units could be formed.

be seen as hypocritical in helping to preserve a practice that they themselves had outlawed decades earlier.

Slavery in America was not to end until the adoption of the Thirteenth Amendment to the Constitution in late 1865, months after the close of the war. By then, several states—Louisiana, Maryland, and Tennessee among them—had already abolished the practice on their own.

On the Western Front: Vicksburg

The first military operation of 1863 took place on the western front. Led by Ulysses S. Grant, it was aimed at Vicksburg on the Mississippi River, and was launched after the general had spent the winter vainly attempting to penetrate the city's defenses.

Vicksburg was a vital target. With the Mississippi's northern and southern reaches in Union hands, the city had become the last open door to the South. Lying on the river's east bank, it received a steady flow of cattle and other goods from the West. That door had to be slammed shut to hasten the day when the Confederacy would be forced to surrender because it was cut off from all outside help.

Grant opened his campaign in late March. From his camp some 20 miles (32 kilometers) north of Vicksburg, he marched 50,000 men down the west side of the Mississippi, well out of the range of the city's massed artillery. At the same time, a fleet of gunboats and barges commanded by Admiral David D. Porter sailed along the river. Porter was to slip past all the enemy batteries, rejoin Grant far to the south, and ferry the troops over to the east bank.

The general held his breath on the night of April 16 when Porter made his run past the city. Though shrouded in darkness, the admiral was sighted, triggering a two-and-a-half-hour rain of shells. As if by miracle, he managed to reach safety with only one gunboat damaged. He then continued south and joined Grant at the town of Bruinsburg. There, at month's end, he began moving the Federals across the river.

This undated photograph of General Grant was taken by Mathew Brady, a photographer who documented much of the war for future generations.

Once on the east bank, Grant did not move immediately to Vicksburg. Rather, he speared inland to the city of Jackson. He routed the Confederate force there and took control of the railroad line that ran to Vicksburg.

With the railroad in his hands and with troops that he had left on guard across the river in his march past the city, Vicksburg was now isolated, cut off from supplies from either the east or west. It was time to attack.

He marched west and, after defeating a Confederate force that came out to intercept him, arrived outside the city on May 18. The next day, and again on May 22, he hit Vicksburg with assaults on its back and side doors. Both attacks were repulsed by enemy artillery and infantry. He then did what he had always suspected the city's heavy defenses would force him to do. He settled down to an artillery siege.

The siege lasted seven weeks. Day and night, Vicksburg cringed under the Union shelling. Homes and buildings were shattered. Hospitals became crowded with the victims of shrapnel and falling brickwork. To protect themselves, families lived in their cellars and came upstairs only to cook or retrieve some needed possession. Those who lost their homes dug caves in which to hide. Food soon ran low and turned the people into dirt-streaked walking skeletons. As the food supply dwindled to nothing, soldiers and civilians alike began killing and eating dogs, cats, and even rats. It was a horror that continued until July 4, when the commander of the Rebel defenses, realizing that all was lost, handed the city over to Grant.

The Mississippi River, from Union territory in the north down to the Gulf of Mexico, was at last totally under Federal control. The Confederacy, already desperately short of arms, uniforms, and even shoes due to Lincoln's blockade and the loss of New Orleans, was doomed to strangle to death.

On the Eastern Front: Chancellorsville

Grant was moving on Vicksburg when the year's first campaign on the eastern front opened. It was launched by Major General Joseph "Fighting Joe" Hooker, who had been given command of the Army of the Potomac after Burnside's tragic waste of men at Fredericksburg.

Hooker was making the Union's fifth stab at Richmond. To reach the city with his 100,000 men, he had to get past

Lee, who was still entrenched at Fredericksburg. He planned to do so by sweeping west of the Rebel positions and hitting them from behind. Then, with Lee trapped, he would drive on to Richmond.

The strategy almost worked. Hooker moved so swiftly that he was already swinging around Lee's western flank when the Confederate general discovered his presence. Lee immediately pulled most of his troops out of Fredericksburg and, with Stonewall Jackson, set out to stop Hooker. The two forces met on May 1 at the tiny hamlet of Chancellorsville in the region of dense woods called the Wilderness.

That night, Lee told Jackson of his plan for ending the thrust at Richmond. Jackson was to do to Hooker what "Fighting Joe" was trying to do to them. He was to sneak 26,000 men around the Union flank and attack from the rear while Lee himself struck from the front.

The next morning Jackson led his infantrymen (who could move so swiftly that he called them his "foot cavalry") on a 12-mile (19-kilometer) march out to the edge of Hooker's line and curled them in behind the Union troops. The Rebels then silently crept through dense woods until they came to an enemy camp late in the afternoon. After watching the Federals prepare their evening meal for a time, they erupted from among the trees, caught the campers completely off guard, and sent them fleeing. Giving chase, the Confederates came to within arm's reach of Hooker's headquarters before Union reserve troops rushed in and turned them away at dusk, putting an end to the day's action.

But the night brought disaster. With a group of officers, Jackson spent several hours riding through the woods to visit his troops. As the riders were returning to their camp, they were suddenly hit by rifle fire from a Confederate unit that mistook them for enemy cavalrymen. Three bullets struck Jackson—one in each hand and the third in his left arm.

His fellow riders carried the general to his camp, where the arm was amputated. He was then taken away to safety. But he fell ill with pneumonia, grew weaker as the days passed, and died on May 10. The death of the man who had become his most able commander affected Lee deeply. Recalling Jackson fondly as an endearing eccentric who imagined he was beset by every conceivable illness and who refused to eat pepper because he was sure it made his left leg hurt, Lee told his officers that he had lost "my good right arm."

By the time of Jackson's death, the battle at Chancellorsville was over and Hooker was in flight. On May 3 and 4, Lee, brilliantly moving his troops to wherever they could do the most harm, battered Hooker from the front while Jackson's men, now commanded by General James E. B. "Jeb" Stuart, harassed him from the rear. When the fighting at last claimed 17,000 Union casualties, Hooker could take no more of the battle. He ordered a retreat and started back toward Washington.

For Lee, though he had suffered 13,000 casualties and lost Jackson, Chancellorsville was his greatest victory of the war. But, for Lincoln, it was a crushing disappointment that sent him in search of a replacement for Hooker.

CHAPTER EIGHT

1863: To the North with Lee—Gettysburg

The Union defeats at Fredericksburg and Chancellorsville inspired Lee to attempt a daring maneuver. He asked Jefferson Davis for permission to invade the North anew and strike again at Pennsylvania. He wanted to demoralize the Union and bolster Southern resolve to continue fighting.

That resolve was weakening, Lee knew. Military supplies were fast dwindling because of the blockade, the people still had enough food for survival, thanks to the South's farms, but the blockade, the loss of New Orleans, and the siege of Vicksburg were depriving them of other necessities for daily life—everything from salt to cloth for badly needed new clothing. The people were sorrowing over lost loved ones. There were whispers of suing for peace. A successful strike on the North could well fend off disaster.

Davis gave his permission, and Lee marched his army, now 75,000 men strong, up into Pennsylvania, reaching a point some 20 miles (32 kilometers) northwest of the small town of Gettysburg in late June. He did not know it at the time, but the Army of the Potomac had come north from Washington to catch him. Commanding the 92,000-man force was Major General George G. Meade, a veteran of Antietam and Fredericksburg who, on Lincoln's orders, had replaced Joseph Hooker.

On June 30, some of Lee's forward troops moved over to scout Gettysburg and accidentally ran into a Federal advance unit. Both sent word to their commanders that they had sighted the enemy, causing Lee and Meade to begin moving toward the small town. Lee, surprised to find his adversary close on his heels, knew that he must make a major stand there. He was confident that the Federals, who had been weakened by Fredericksburg and Chancellorsville, would not be up to such a battle.

If he could crush the Army of the Potomac once and for all, he could swing about and speed back to Washington. Should the capital then fall to him, he would do far more than turn the fighting around for the Confederacy. He would force Lincoln to negotiate for peace in the South's favor.

The stage was set that June 30 for the most monumental battle of the war. It would rage for three terrible days.

Gettysburg: Day One

Early on July 1, the first of Lee's arriving men attacked the enemy advance unit, which was now located just to the north of Gettysburg. Only a few shots were exchanged, but as the day wore on and both armies began appearing on the scene, the fighting intensified. Lee sent troops against the Union advance unit and drove its men back through Gettysburg, with the Federals finally settling into a defensive position in the hills south of town. The main body of Meade's army joined them there that night.

These new arrivals quickly spread out along a front 3 miles (5 kilometers) long. Digging in on high ground so that they could fire down on an attack, they set up a line that started in the south at a hill called Little Round Top, ran northward along a rise known as Cemetery Ridge, and curved eastward across Cemetery and Culp Hills in front of Gettysburg.

That same night, Lee positioned his own troops. He placed Longstreet, who had become his chief aide since Stonewall Jackson's death, along a line facing Little Round

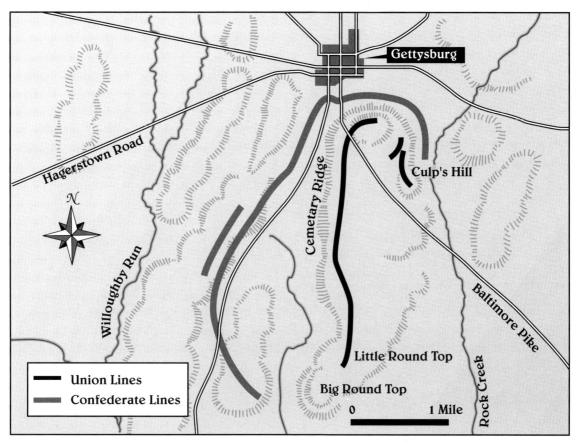

THE BATTLE OF GETTYSBURG

Top and Cemetery Ridge, both about a mile distant. Other units were stationed between Gettysburg and the Federals on Cemetery and Culp Hills. Lee did not like to see the Federals holding the high ground, but, weakened as they were, he was sure he could drive them into a rout.

Gettysburg: Day Two

On the second day, Lee attacked the southern and northern ends of the Federal line. The southern assault was handled by James Longstreet, whose line was separated from Little Round Top by a thick woods and then an open area. When he emerged from the woods, he found that the Federals had left Little Round Top and had come forward to dig in at three points—in a peach orchard and adjoining wheat field, and along a road that ran north to Gettysburg. The shift had been made because their commander felt it gave them a better defensive position.

Though many of his men were still on somewhat elevated ground, the move proved to be a disastrous mistake—because Robert E. Lee had spread his force too thin. Longstreet took full advantage of the error. He struck savagely with his artillery and infantry. In seesaw fighting, the Federals were driven back to an area cluttered with boulders, near the base of Little Round Top. Here, the battle became a deadly rifle duel. Both the Union and Rebel soldiers darted from rock to rock and then took aim at any figure that loomed in front of them. Everywhere, men fell with gunshot wounds. The Federals soon gave the place a grim name: Devil's Den.

This rebel sharpshooter lost his life at Devil's Den along with many other young men.

The fight to clear Devil's Den went so slowly that, at times, it seemed to be stalled. But, inch by inch, the Federals retreated until their backs were against the base of Little Round Top. At that time, one of Meade's commanders, General Gouverneur Warren, galloped to the hilltop to survey the fighting below.

Shocked at what he saw, he immediately went in search of reinforcements for the hilltop. He brought back an infantry outfit and an artillery battery. The artillerymen wrestled their cannon up the hillside and, with the infantry, opened fire on the Confederates coming out of Devil's Den, ending the danger to Little Round Top. Had the hill fallen to the Confederates, the Battle of Gettysburg would likely have ended in victory for them. They would have been able to rake Meade's troops on Cemetery Ridge with cannon fire.

A little later, Federal units were sent to Big Round Top, which stood just south of Little Round Top and had not been previously manned by defenders. With both Round Tops in Union hands, the southern end of Meade's line was safe and secure.

Up at the north end of the line, the troops on Cemetery Ridge and Cemetery and Culp Hills came under heavy attacks. Though taking heavy losses and though almost overwhelmed at several points, they held their ground, doing so at times with their bayonets. By day's end, all the Union positions were still intact, but tattered and reduced in strength.

Gettysburg: Day Three

On the third day, Lee decided to loose a full-scale assault at the center of the Union line on Cemetery Ridge. The decision appalled Longstreet. He vehemently argued that the troops would be committing suicide when they crossed the open area in front of the Ridge. The Federals would rip them to pieces from their elevated positions. But Lee, still certain that the Federals would have no stomach for a major fight and would crack and flee, shook his head at what was a very commonsense argument.

And so, at 1:00 P.M, he massed all his artillery—totaling more than 140 cannons—and unleashed a two-hour barrage on the Ridge. Firing nonstop and blanketing the Ridge with black smoke, the guns ripped up Union infantry positions and artillery emplacements. The Federals returned the fire, but failed to silence the barrage.

At 3:00 P.M., the Rebel artillery suddenly fell silent. Up on the Ridge, the battered Union soldiers, stunned but not broken by the barrage, looked down on the spectacle of a wall of gray emerging from the woods in front of the enemy lines. The Rebel troops, 15,000 in all, moved with calm precision as they formed a line facing the Ridge, a line that stretched for more than a mile by the time every man was in place.

Then, with the same precision, they began to cross the open ground leading to the base of the Ridge. Spearheading the move were contingents of infantry commanded by Major General George E. Pickett. Because of their leading position, the advance was to be remembered always as "Pickett's Charge."

Meade's artillery quickly set its sights on the approaching troops. Shells began to burst among the attackers. Gaping holes appeared in their line. Everywhere, gray-uniformed men fell and were instantly replaced by the comrades behind them. The artillery switched from shells to cannisters, tin cans packed with iron slugs that were hurled in all directions when the containers exploded. Greater holes appeared in the gray line, and then became yet greater when the Confederates moved within range of the Union rifles. To make matters worse, Union contingents at either end of the line slipped forward and began shredding it from the side. Still the Rebel tide flowed

On November 19, 1863, the battlefield where so many of the dead of both sides lay buried was dedicated as a National Cemetery. At the close of the ceremony, which was attended by some 20,000 people, President Lincoln dedicated the site with a 272-word speech that has been admired ever since as one of the finest and most eloquent examples of oratory in the English language, the Gettysburg Address:

Fourscore and seven years ago our fathers brought forth on this continent a new nation, conceived in liberty and dedicated to the proposition that all men are created equal. Now we are engaged in a great civil war, testing whether that nation or any nation so conceived and so dedicated can long endure. We are met on a great battlefield of that war. We have come to dedicate a portion of that field as a final resting-place for those who gave their lives that that nation might live. It is altogether fitting and proper that we should do this. But in a larger sense, we cannot dedicate, we cannot consecrate, we cannot hallow this ground. The brave men, living and dead who struggled here have consecrated it far above our poor power to add or detract. The world will little note nor long remember what we say here, but it can never forget what they did here. It is for us the living rather to be dedicated here to the unfinished work which they who fought here have thus far so nobly advanced. It is rather for us to be here dedicated to the great task remaining before us—that from these honored dead we take increased devotion to the cause for which they gave the last full measure of devotion—that we here highly resolve that these dead shall not have died in vain, that this nation under God shall have a new birth of freedom, and that government of the people, by the people, for the people shall not perish from the earth.

onward, at last reaching the base of Cemetery Ridge and beginning to struggle upward.

Now the Union rifles began to fire at almost point-blank range, sending their targets toppling over backward. But the Confederates stubbornly went on climbing. Then they were crashing in among the Federals. Screaming and cursing, men threw themselves at each other, firing blindly, lashing out with rifle butts, and lunging at each other with bayonets.

The Confederates had made their way to the Union defenses, yes, but now they were too exhausted to hold their prize. They suddenly seemed to realize this and, just as suddenly, the fighting ended. Swamped by the enemy, 4,000 of their number threw down their arms while others stumbled away and began to stagger back to their own lines.

With their retreat, the fighting at Gettysburg ended in catastrophe for Lee. Chancellorsville had been his greatest victory, but Gettysburg now stood as his greatest defeat, costing him 28,000 troops—more than one third of his army. The survivors were exhausted, their uniforms filthy, their shoes in tatters. And, with their rations almost gone, they were on the point of starvation.

On July 4, the same day that Vicksburg fell into Grant's hands far to the west, Lee, knowing he could advance no farther, set up camp some distance behind the battlefront and then ordered a retreat home to Virginia.

In the White House, Lincoln received word of the two great victories. But he looked on Gettysburg as a defeat because of Meade's behavior following the battle. The general, with 23,000 casualties but with an army still far outnumbering Lee's, had not struck at the bedraggled enemy to win what could have been a war-ending victory. Instead, he had rested his troops for a week before moving on Lee's encampment, only to find that the Confederates had departed south and escaped back to Virginia. Once again, a general had failed the President. Lincoln still needed a leader who could have the Union troops fight on, no matter how tired or badly mauled.

On the Western Front

After Gettysburg, the principal action of 1863 was seen on the western front, in Tennessee. Continuing there was the fighting that had started in December 1862, when Confederate and Union forces battled to a draw at Murfreesboro and then retired into winter quarters.

The first half of the year was spent in Union efforts to oust General Braxton Bragg from Tennessee. He was pushed back to Chattanooga and then driven from the city in late summer. Trailed by 58,000 Federals, he retreated into northwestern Georgia, where he turned to challenge them at Chickamauga Creek. In fighting that raged through September 19 and 20, both sides absorbed stunning losses: 16,170 casualties for the Union, and 18,464 for the South. But, despite suffering the greater number of losses, Bragg emerged the victor. The Federals fell back to Chattanooga, after which Bragg lay siege to the city.

Lincoln had just placed Grant in command of all the forces on the western front. In October, the general moved from Vicksburg and took command of the Federals at Chattanooga. He ejected Bragg from the city and pushed him over to Lookout Mountain. There and at Missionary Ridge, where Bragg had established his headquarters, the Union men defeated the Rebels and sent them retreating into Georgia. All Confederates were at last gone from Tennessee. The state was securely under Union control.

Lookout Mountain and Missionary Ridge convinced Lincoln that, as he had long suspected, Grant was the very general he needed to fight on, no matter the consequences. Here was the man who had suffered defeats when first trying to pierce the defenses at Vicksburg but had doggedly stuck to his attack until the city was his. With the Confederacy now hemmed in from the west and, as always, from the north, here was the man whose unwavering determination could finally win the war.

The President called Grant to Washington and appointed him general-in-chief of all the Union armies.

CHAPTER NINE

1864–1865: To Appomattox Court House

Ulysses S. Grant assumed his duties as general-in-chief in March 1864. His task now was to invade the South and destroy two armies: Lee's 60,000-man Army of Northern Virginia, which was safeguarding Richmond, and a 55,000-man force on watch at Atlanta, Georgia.

The years of fighting had taken a terrible toll on the Confederate troops. In 1863 alone, they had sustained well over 100,000 casualties. The Confederacy was running out of men. The Virginia and Georgia armies were its last major forces. Crush them, Grant knew, and the war would be won.

He was to strike with two armies. He himself would lead the Army of the Potomac against Lee at Richmond, while a force under General William Tecumseh Sherman would sweep down on Atlanta.

The Virginia Campaign, 1864

With 120,000 men, Grant entered Virginia as May dawned. His line of march led him into the dense woods where the Battle of Chancellorsville had been fought—the Wilderness. There, on May 5, he came under attack by Lee.

When Lee had heard that Grant was on the move, he was faced with two choices: stay where he was and defend Richmond or go on the offensive. He opted for the latter, electing to strike in the Wilderness because he knew that the Union artillery, far outnumbering his, would be hampered by the densely packed trees.

The attack opened the vicious struggle known as the Battle of the Wilderness. On both sides, soldiers blindly struggled among the trees in the choking smoke created by the gunfire. Most often, all they could see were the flashes of rifles firing from behind tree trunks and the underbrush. They fought in such close quarters at times that their rifles were fired when muzzle to muzzle. All the

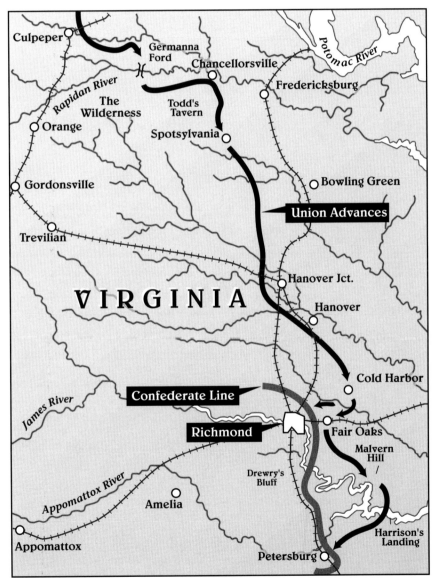

ULYSSES S. GRANT AND ROBERT E. LEE, HEAD-TO-HEAD

bloodshed gained neither side an inch of ground, but cost Grant some 17,000 losses and Lee approximately 12,000.

To break the deadlock and continue toward Richmond, Grant broke off the battle at the close of its second day and skirted around the Confederates' eastern flank. Quickly, Lee followed with a blocking move. It brought the two armies up against each other some miles south at the village of Spotsylvania. Savage face-to-face fighting continued until mid-month.

Again, Grant ended matters with a skirting maneuver. He moved now to the town of Cold Harbor, located a short distance northeast of Richmond. Again, Lee followed, careful always to keep himself between the enemy and Richmond. The two forces clashed once more when they reached Cold Harbor, where, in early June, Grant threw his troops against a Rebel position so heavily fortified that it cost him some 7,000 men.

By now, Grant had sustained 31,000 casualties. He regretted the death and suffering, but the number of the lost did not frighten him. He knew he could call in reinforcements from Washington, while every Rebel casualty reduced the size of Lee's army. Grant claimed that he could lose two men to every one lost by Lee and still emerge victorious.

With yet another skirting maneuver, Grant abandoned Cold Harbor. He marched across York Peninsula, and, in mid-June, settled in at Petersburg, about 25 miles (40 kilometers) southeast of Richmond. He immediately attacked the town, but was repulsed by the arriving Lee and the troops already stationed there.

Denied entry to Petersburg, Grant began a siege of the town, while Lee established a defensive line stretching 20 miles toward Richmond. In addition, the Confederate general dispatched a force northward to harass the area near Washington, D.C., hoping that Grant would send some of his men chasing in pursuit. Commanded by Lieutenant General Jubal Early, the Rebels came so close to the capital that they were able to bombard its outer defenses—so close, in fact, that one sharpshooter fired on Lincoln when the President came out to inspect the defenses one day.

As Lee had hoped, Grant ordered troops under Major General Philip Sheridan to find Early. But the outcome proved a disappointment for Lee. Sheridan raced north, located Early in the Shenandoah Valley, and defeated him in October, putting an end to the threat on Washington and bringing Sheridan back to Petersburg.

All the while, Grant continued his siege of Petersburg and the Rebel defensive line. It was to continue until the spring of 1865.

Sherman into Georgia, 1864

In early May, Sherman departed Chattanooga, Tennessee, with 100,000 troops and entered Georgia in quest of Atlanta. Facing him were 55,000 Confederates under General Joseph Johnston, who had been wounded while defending Richmond during the Peninsular Campaign and who had now replaced Bragg after the defeat at Lookout Mountain. Up against an enemy twice his size, Johnston could do little but slow the Union advance, a job he performed splendidly. He fell back slowly before the invaders, taking defensive positions in the best spots available and holding them for as long as possible before retreating again. His finest moment came on Kenesaw Mountain where, on June 27, his tenacious stand so exasperated Sherman that the Union general hit him with a frontal attack—and lost 3,000 men.

After Kenesaw Mountain, Johnston abandoned his delaying tactics, knowing them to be futile. He retreated to Atlanta to solidify the defenses there. The sudden retreat angered Jefferson Davis, who had expected Johnston to stop Sherman. Davis removed Johnston from command and replaced him with General John Hood, a Texan still eager to fight despite losing an arm at Gettysburg and a leg at Chickamauga.

Once past Kenesaw Mountain, Sherman advanced steadily on toward Atlanta. When the Union troops came within sight of the city, General Hood, a courageous but rash officer, rushed out to battle them on July 20 and 22, and again on July 28. Overwhelmed on each occasion, he stumbled back inside the Atlanta defenses.

Sherman reached Atlanta's outskirts at month's end and placed the city under a siege throughout August. At the same time, he sent columns around to its back door to isolate it from the outside world. Once surrounded, Hood admitted that a further defense of the city was hopeless. He abandoned Atlanta, but with a definite plan as to how he would continue fighting.

With Hood gone, Sherman entered the city on September 2. He was now determined to quell the South not only by defeating its troops but also by demoralizing its people and destroying its agricultural and industrial facilities. To begin this strategy, he expelled Atlanta's entire civilian population, saying that, if the Southerners wanted peace, "they and their relatives must stop the war."

Once out of Atlanta, Hood put his plan for his next move into effect. He thrust north to harass Sherman's supply line, which extended all the way back to Chattanooga. His hope was to anger Sherman into leaving Atlanta and chasing after him. But Sherman did not take the bait. Rather, he sent 60,000 troops under General George Thomas to deal with Hood.

Sherman did intend to leave Atlanta, but not in the way Hood had hoped. He now planned to march some 300 miles (483 kilometers) southeast to the city of Savannah on the Atlantic coast and split Georgia in half. As he marched, he would employ his strategy of demoralizing the people and wrecking the area's farming and industry. From there, he would swing north through the Carolinas and join Grant in Virginia for a final death strike at Richmond.

Wherever he now went, the general with the skull-like, deeply lined face would wreak havoc. Left always in his wake would be charred towns, blazing farms, scorched

Lincoln's second inauguration, March 4, 1865.

In the 1864 presidential election, Abraham Lincoln won a second term in the White House. To the President, the victory seemed a miracle. His popularity with the Northern public had plunged to an alarming low before the election, and he had seemed doomed to defeat at the hands of his opponent—the man who had once so annoyed him, "Tardy George" McClellan.

Why had the President's popularity fallen? First, many Northerners had been angered over the terms of the Emancipation Proclamation. The abolitionists thought them too weak, while proslavery supporters regarded them as too strong.

(continued)

Further, the great victories at Antietam and Gettysburg had been forgotten. Myriad voters had felt that the President was allowing the war to drag on too long and that it might well end in defeat for the Union. Grant was bogged down at Petersburg and had lost thousands of men while fighting in the Wilderness. There was sorrow at his losses and anger at his willingness to sacrifice so many men in his quest for Richmond—and anger at Lincoln for letting him do so.

But then there was an abrupt change of mind. With Sherman's capture of Atlanta, thousands of Northerners again thought that the Union could triumph after all. They returned Lincoln to the White House to finish his war work. Thereafter, the President would credit his success at the polls to Sherman.

Once reelected, Lincoln threw his support to the Thirteenth Amendment to the Constitution, the one that would end slavery in the nation once and for all. The amendment took effect in late 1865, eight months after the war's end, when ratified by the states.

fields, and uprooted railroad tracks. With these actions, the officer who friends knew as warm-hearted became the most hated figure in the South.

To make sure that Atlanta would never serve the Confederacy again, Sherman put the city to the torch before leaving. Flames shot skyward as his troops detonated warehouses, ammunition dumps, machine shops, and public buildings. Several hundred Atlanta acres lay in ashes by the time he was finished.

The general began his march to Savannah—or, as the press called it, his "March to the Sea"—on November 15. A month later, he was closing in on the city. Behind him was a 60-mile (96-kilometer) -wide path of ruin carved by his men as, far out-running their supply line, they had stripped the land of food and had set fields, villages, roadside inns, farmhouses, barns, corrals, wagons, and even plows afire.

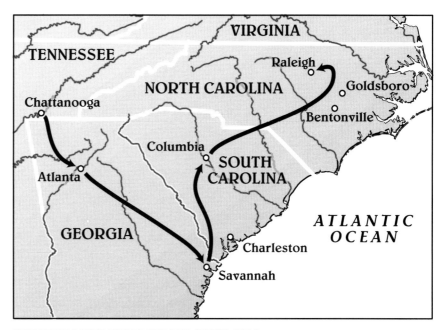

SHERMAN'S MARCH TO THE SEA

As he was nearing his destination, Sherman learned that General Thomas had pursued Hood up to Tennessee, where on December 15–16, he had defeated the Rebels and hurled them back into Georgia. The pleased general took Savannah on December 21 without a fight and ended his work for the year.

Sherman's Last Battles, 1865

Soon after 1865 dawned, Sherman was again on the march, this time moving toward the Carolinas. Facing him as he departed Savannah in early February were the remnants of Hood's army. On returning to Georgia after his Tennessee failure, Hood had been dismissed by Jefferson Davis, who had then handed the troops back to Joseph Johnston. Johnston had sped eastward to stand once again in Sherman's path.

As usual, Johnston, with his troops now numbering fewer than 40,000, could do nothing but fight a series of delaying actions. They did little to slow Sherman as he swept through South Carolina and pushed into North Carolina, coming at last to the town of Bentonville. There, Johnston made an all-out stand against the surging Federals. The fighting lasted from March 19 to 21, and its outcome was as expected. Though inflicting heavy losses on the Federals, Johnston staggered back in retreat. His final battle in the war was ended.

From Bentonville, Sherman moved to Goldsboro, where he established his headquarters, later to send his troops into Raleigh. At Goldsboro, he was just 150 miles (241 kilometers) from Richmond and ready to move to Grant's side.

But the chance to move never came. Late that March, a series of events began to unfold at Petersburg. They were to bring the war to a close in a mere sixteen days.

The Death of Richmond, 1865

The nine-month siege of Petersburg had cost Lee dearly in troops. Adding to his losses were his men from Georgia and the Carolinas. They shuddered at the news of what Sherman was doing to their states. Daily, in increasing numbers, they deserted Lee and rushed home to help their loved ones. General Robert E. Lee was now down to 30,000 troops and facing 113,000 Federals. Knowing that he could not stand still while his army dwindled away to nothing, he undertook a daring and ill-fated move.

On March 25, he sent advance troops charging out of Petersburg in an attempt to cut a gap through the Union's eastern flank so that the rest of his army could pour through it and escape to North Carolina. He would join Johnston and defeat Sherman. Then, together, they would hit Grant.

The stratagem almost worked. His advance troops took Fort Stedman just east of Petersburg and began to open the needed pathway to freedom. But, as had happened long ago at Fort Donelson, Grant swiftly counterattacked, closed the gap, and sent the Rebels reeling back to Petersburg.

It was now Grant's turn to take the offensive. He had been planning a full-scale assault on Lee's line for days, but had not been able to act because of heavy rains. Now, with the weather clearing, he staged a preliminary action that sent Philip Sheridan's troops dashing to the end of Lee's defenses near Richmond. Spearing in behind them, Sheridan captured the spot known as Five Forks on April 1 and took over a railroad to keep Lee from using it to make a quick retreat when Grant's main attack was unleashed.

That attack came the next morning. Grant hurled his entire army all along the length of Lee's line. The Rebels hadn't the manpower to resist the thousands of Federals who came charging at them at dawn. The attackers quickly carved gaping holes in the line and poured through them, driving thousands of Confederates to flee—some toward Petersburg and some toward Richmond.

Lee, watching the tragedy, sent a message to Jefferson Davis, urging him to leave Richmond and saying that he himself must soon abandon Petersburg. Davis took the advice and fled with his government that night, traveling 100 miles (160 kilometers) southwest to the town of Danville. The people of Richmond, learning of his departure, panicked. By the thousands, fighting each other for wagons and carriages in which to carry their belongings, they joined his flight. Soldiers began to blow up arsenals and the bridges across the James River to keep vital stores out of Grant's hands and to hinder his entry into the city. The explosions triggered fires that raced from street to street and bathed the dark sky in a deep red.

That same night, Lee evacuated Petersburg. Mustering as many troops as possible, he moved southwest through an area left open by the attacking Federals, his hope now being to reach Davis at Danville and then slip into the nearby mountains, where he could continue fighting indefinitely.

But Grant came snapping at his heels, attacking Lee's columns from the rear and thinning his fleeing ranks to fewer than 10,000 men in the next days. Lee, hating what was happening but still loyally fighting for the South, refused to be stopped by the attacks. But, on April 8, near a spot called Appomattox Court House, he learned that Union troops had slipped past him and had surrounded his starving and haggard men. He ordered a final desperate effort to break through the Union net. When it failed, his shoulders sagged with an awful weariness. There was nothing more he could do but meet with Grant.

The Last Day, April 9, 1865

Early on Palm Sunday, April 9, Lee donned his finest uniform, mounted his beloved horse, Traveler, and rode into Appomattox Court House under a white flag. His men and Sheridan's Federals had been about to do battle there, but, on learning of Lee's approach, had been ordered not to open fire. The men of both sides, knowing that something momentous was happening, stood watching as Lee rode to a house owned by Wilmer McLean.

Grant arrived at Appomattox Court House a short time later, having been informed that Lee was awaiting him there. When Sheridan pointed to the McLean house, Grant swung toward it, dismounted, and entered its front parlor. After months of struggle, he and Lee at last faced each other, Lee resplendent in his uniform and Grant filthy and mud-caked because he had been in the field all night.

The two sat down and quietly discussed the terms of surrender. Knowing that the end was near, Grant and Lincoln had met some days earlier to develop the terms, which now proved to be generous. All Confederate military stores were to be surrendered; Lee's troops—officers and men alike—were to be paroled and were to promise not to take up arms again until properly exchanged; his cavalry and artillery officers, all of whom owned their horses, were to be allowed to keep them. Though that final term referred only to officers, Grant said that he would "let all men who claim to own a horse or a mule take the animals home with them to work their little farms."

Head-Quarters, Appomattox C.H. Va.
Apl. 9th 1865, 4.30 o'clock, P M.

Hon. E. M. Stanton, Sec. of War Washington
Gen. Lee surrendered the Army of Northern Va this afternoon on terms proposed by myself. The accompanying additional correspondence will show the conditions fully.

U. S. Grant
Lt. Gen.

9 ~ Apl '65 —

Gen'l
    I have rec'd your note of this date. Though not entertaining the opinion you express of the hopelessness of further resistance on the part of the Army of N. Va — I reciprocate your desire to avoid useless effusion of blood, I therefore before considering your proposition ask the terms you will offer on condition of its surrender
            Very resp'y your Ob't Se'v't
                R E Lee
                Gen'l

Lt. Gen'l U. S. Grant
Comm'd Armies of the U. States

After General Grant accepted Lee's surrender (right) on Sunday afternoon, April 9, he was riding to his headquarters when he realized he had not notified the government. He promptly sat down and wrote this note (above).

After outlining the terms, Grant put them in writing. Lee then read them through and wrote a short letter of acceptance. Finally he stood, shook hands with Grant, nodded to the officers of both sides gathered in the room, and walked out the front door. He paused for a long moment in the warm sunlight and looked at the mixture of gray- and blue-uniformed men who were gathered all about—a blend of men who had followed him faithfully and men who had fought him courageously. At last, his voice low and choking, he called for Traveler, mounted to the saddle, and slowly rode away.

Over in North Carolina, General Johnston would not surrender until April 26, and there would be sporadic fighting elsewhere until May. But, with Lee's acceptance of the surrender terms on this Palm Sunday of 1865, four long years of a nation at war with itself were at an end.

EPILOGUE

The Aftermath

The fighting was over. Left in its wake were at least 1.04 million Americans dead and wounded. Union losses came to some 360,000 dead and over 275,000 wounded. Due to the havoc wrought in the South, the number of Confederate casualties is uncertain. It is estimated, though, that they totaled at least 275,000 dead and 100,000 wounded.

Great areas of the South lay in ruins. Decades were needed to build a new South from those ruins. Some restoration, however, was completed quickly. Within six months of the war's end, the burned Atlanta was much rebuilt and the production of cotton had returned to prewar levels. But the rebirth of other cities took years. And a quarter century passed before Southern livestock were restored to their 1861 numbers.

Though the nation was again united, American life was profoundly changed. Hatreds ignited by the war were to flame for generations. In the minds of many of the descendants of the men who fought, they remain smoldering to this day.

Life was profoundly changed in other ways. For one, the North became the nation's predominant economic region. For another, after causing so much North-South friction over the years, the idea of states' rights was now greatly weakened. The nation had been reunited as a union with a strong central government. Made secondary to that union was the power of the individual states.

The end of the fighting marked the beginning of the period called Reconstruction, the time in which the South was to be rebuilt and returned to the Union. Abraham Lincoln had hoped the period would be governed by a policy of "malice toward none...charity for all." Had he lived, it is likely that he would have won congressional support for this policy.

But, tragically, he did not live, and Reconstruction was marked by stern Union policies that struck the Southerners as punishment. The former Confederate states were placed under the tight control of Federal troops. Because certain Northern politicians hoped to build a black voting bloc favorable to their views, Washington took local political power away from the whites and handed it to freed slaves who, uneducated, were ill-equipped to handle it. Greedy Northerners (and some Southerners) supported them, all for the purpose of reaping great wealth through graft and corruption. The situation enraged the South, with much of the fury being directed at the former slaves.

When the Federal troops departed in 1877, marking the end of Reconstruction, the white Southerners again won local political control and, in a variety of ways, began to render the ex-slaves powerless. For example, with a series of regulations, such as the requirement that one could cast a ballot only if able to read and write, they took away the blacks' right to vote.

Over the years, while many ex-slaves remained working on the plantations where they had spent their lives, thousands of blacks abandoned the South and moved first to the industrial North in search of employment and then to every corner of the nation.

All the above factors, each having to do with the absorption of the former slaves and their descendants into the mainstream of American life, caused old prejudices and hatreds to flame high. Sadly, those flames still burn today, though we can hope that we are approaching the time when they may finally be extinguished.

Abraham Lincoln

Widely hailed as the nation's greatest president because of his successful efforts to preserve the Union, Abraham Lincoln survived the war by less than a week. On April 14, 1865, while attending a play, *Our American Cousin*, at Ford's Theatre in Washington, he was shot and fatally wounded by actor John Wilkes Booth, a fanatical Southern sympathizer. The President lingered for hours and died the following morning, at the age of fifty-six.

Jefferson Davis

A member of both the U.S. House of Representatives and the Senate prior to the war, Jefferson Davis spent two years in prison following Lee's surrender. In the eyes of myriad Southerners, his imprisonment made him a martyr to the Confederate cause. His final years were given to a number of failed business ventures. He was eighty-one years old when he died in 1889.

Ulysses S. Grant

Following the war, Ulysses S. Grant served as secretary of war under President Andrew Johnson and then, in 1869, entered the White House as the nation's eighteenth president, remaining there for two terms. In his later years, he wrote his autobiography in two volumes, *Personal Memoirs of U. S. Grant*. His death, at the age of sixty-three, came in 1885 and was caused by throat cancer.

Robert E. Lee

Robert E. Lee was named commander of all Confederate forces in the closing days of the war, too late for him to change the course of the fighting. In the postwar years, Lee served as president of Virginia's Washington College (today Washington and Lee University) and, at the same time, worked to rebuild the South. He died in 1870, also at the age of sixty-three.

In time, the American Civil War became known as the first of the modern wars, a well-deserved title. Brought to bear during the fighting were weapons (some of which had been tried on a limited basis in earlier conflicts) that became all too familiar in future battles, among them the breech-loading rifle, hand grenades, barbed wire, and booby traps. The war's ironclad ships marked the passing of the wooden warship and changed naval warfare for all time to come.

The greatest change, however, was surely the military's shift away from attempting to dominate an enemy by destroying his army to the strategy of winning by destroying the opponent's economy. As practiced by Sherman, the strategy was not intended to injure or kill civilians but to demoralize them. In later years, civilian populations were to join military personnel as targets for death. We saw this strategy at its most brutal in World War II, in Hitler's blitzkrieg ("lightning war") technique and in the Allied and Axis air bombings of enemy cities.

As the first of the modern wars, the American Civil War was the first conflict to be extensively photographed. Due to the efforts of photographer Mathew Brady and his team of cameramen, we have the first realistic pictorial record of a war. Because they worked with extended exposure times, Brady's team could not create a record of battles in progress. Rather, what has come down to us are stark black-and-white scenes of the devastation left behind by the fighting—torn fields and buildings and the dead lying where they fell. It is a far more memorable record than any battlefield artist of earlier days could ever provide.

It is well that these photographs have been passed down to us, that the bitter memories of the war remain with us, and that we remember how that war sired the horrors of modern warfare. All these factors combine, in a world torn by civil strife, to warn us of the tragedy that could be ours should we ever permit our nation to become again, in Abraham Lincoln's eloquent phrasing, a "house divided."

BIBLIOGRAPHY

Boatner, Mark Mayo III. *The Civil War Dictionary*, revised edition. New York: McKay, 1959.

Burns, Ken. *The Civil War* (a television documentary), Public Broadcasting Service, 1994.

Carruth, Gorton. *The Encyclopedia of American Facts and Dates*, ninth edition. New York: HarperCollins, 1993.

Catton, Bruce. *Gettysburg: The Final Fury*. New York: Doubleday, 1974.

————. *The American Heritage Picture History of the Civil War*, two volumes. New York: American Heritage, 1960.

————. *Mr. Lincoln's Army*. New York: Doubleday, 1951.

————. *A Stillness at Appomattox*. New York: Doubleday, 1951.

Davis, Kenneth C. *Don't Know Much About the Civil War: Everything You Need to Know About America's Greatest Conflict But Never Learned*. New York: William Morrow, 1996.

Garraty, John A. *1,001 Things Everyone Should Know About American History*. New York: Doubleday, 1989.

Hansen, Harry. *The Civil War: A History*. New York: Penguin Books, 1961.

Leckie, Robert. *The Wars of America*, Volume 2: From 1600 to 1900. New York: HarperCollins, 1992.

McPherson, James M. *Battle Cry of Freedom*. New York: Oxford University Press, 1988.

Meltzer, Milton, editor. *Voices from the Civil War: A Documentary History of the Great American Conflict*. New York: Crowell, 1989.

Nevins, Allan, and Commager, Henry Steele. *A Short History of the United States*, fifth edition. New York: The Modern Library, 1966.

Robertson, James I., Jr. *Civil War! America Becomes One Nation*. New York: Knopf, 1992.